THUNDERFIRE

When Chris Ranson inherited his grandfather's ranch, there were unscrupulous forces at work in the territory. Envious eyes had always been cast on the ranch, but old man Ranson's reputation as a gunman had made most men think twice about risking their necks in a gunfight. This new owner, though, was different. According to the stories going around, he was more used to spending his time in the cantinas south of the border than in learning how to handle a gun. Then Chris Ranson buckled on his grandfather's guns . . .

RALPH C. SUMMERS

THUNDERFIRE

Complete and Unabridged

LINFORD
Leicester

First hardcover edition published in
Great Britain in 2003 by
Robert Hale Limited, London

Originally published in paperback as
Thunderfire by Tex Bradley

First Linford Edition
published 2005
by arrangement with
Robert Hale Limited, London

The moral right of the author has been asserted

British Library CIP Data

Summers, Ralph C.
  Thunderfire.—Large print ed.—
Linford western library
1. Western stories
2. Large type books
I. Title II. Bradley, Tex, 1928 –
823.9′14 [F]

ISBN 1–84395–610–1

Published by
F. A. Thorpe (Publishing)
Anstey, Leicestershire

Set by Words & Graphics Ltd.
Anstey, Leicestershire
Printed and bound in Great Britain by
T. J. International Ltd., Padstow, Cornwall

This book is printed on acid-free paper

1

Legacy

It was mid-morning when Chris Ranson forded the wide river that cut across the trail. Back in the night, he had made camp among the tall ridges which overlooked the trail into Memphis, had spent long, shivering, uncomfortable hours in the rocks, hungry and angry at having to be there at all. The letter which had brought him all this way across the wilderness of desert and mountain from the warm country south of the Rio Grande, still reposed in his pocket, a strange letter from the lawyer here in Memphis, asking him to come as quickly as possible. What could any lawyer want with him? he wondered as he off-saddled on the far bank of the slow-flowing river, let his horse blow and drink; and why the urgency so clearly implied in the letter? There had been nothing in it to give him any clear indication of why his presence here was so necessary, merely the tersely worded summons to Memphis.

He seated himself wearily on a low knoll of ground, in the shade of a tall tree which overhung the water, took the letter from his pocket, extracted the paper and read it through once again, trying to read something into it. The wind which swept along the river was good, its smell clean and fresh in his nostrils, but he was anxious to get on and ten minutes later, he tightened the cinch and stepped up into the saddle, turning his mount towards the wide Memphis trail. Tall, broad-shouldered, narrow hipped, his face tanned by the hot Mexican sun, his eyes hard and blue like chips of agate, stared straight ahead of him as he rode. At first sight, he might have been one of a hundred saddle tramps who rode these trails, keeping one uneasy jump ahead of the law, doing a little cowpunching here and there along the way but never stopping for very long in one place. But a closer look would have revealed that the clothes he wore, dusty and travel-stained as they were, were of a different cut to those worn by the ordinary trail-riders. There was an expensive quality about them, the way they had been so obviously tailored to fit him. There was, too, one other thing which marked him out from the usual run of trail trash. He carried no gun in his belt and the Winchester thrust into the saddle scabbard was brand new, shining, the metal glinting brilliantly in the hot sun.

It was high noon when Chris Ranson rode into the streets of Memphis. Heat had come to the town. Heat from the sun and the stretching plains around it. It shimmered in the streets and lay in a heavy, oppressive pressure on the tall buildings that flanked the streets. Siesta time and there were few people abroad at this hour. A handful of

3

ponies stood with a stolid patience, tethered to the hitching rail outside one of the saloons, tails twitching at the flies which had settled in swarms around them. A couple of men drifted slowly across the dusty street towards the nearby hotel, paused for a moment to watch the tall stranger who rode along the street, then turned and pushed open the doors, going inside, out of the heat and the flaming sunlight.

Ranson rode slowly, eyes glancing along the rows of buildings. This was much the same as a score of towns he had seen both north and south of the Rio Grande. Memphis was a town that had been built in a great hurry, sprouting from the desert in the space of a few short months, thrown up by men who were in a hurry to build, to get things done, because the frontiers were pushing south and west and there had to be places such as this to keep things moving, to bring up the freight and the wagon trains, to drive the railroad west, to bring the banks and also law and order into a lawless territory.

He located the livery stable halfway along the street, put in his horse, then turned back, retracing his steps to where he had noticed the lawyer's office, the faded gilt lettering over the doorway peeled off by the action of sun and rain and the driving, abrading dust that blew along the street. He thrust open the door with the flat of his hand, walked in with the assurance of a man used to having things done his way. The office was empty as he entered, and he could feel the tremendous heat of the sun strike his shoulders through the dusty, fly-speckled window that looked out on to the wide street. In spite of the bright sunlight that streamed through the window, the room still contrived to look dark and forbidding. Maybe it was the furniture that did it, he reflected, glancing about him. The heavy, solid, carved woodenness of it, with the huge desk dominating everything.

The door at the back of the room opened and Ranson turned quickly, facing the man who stepped through. Lawyer Sims was a small man, his face lined and wizened so that it was virtually impossible to guess at his real age. He peered closely at Ranson through the rimless glasses perched on the end of his thin nose, then moved to the desk and stood behind it, as if it afforded him some form of protection.

'I'm Chris Ranson.' He took the letter from his pocket and held it out to the other, leaning forward over the desk as he did so.

'You got here fast,' acknowledged the other. He seated himself in the padded chair at the back of the desk, motioned Chris to the other. 'I didn't expect you for some days yet, wasn't even sure that my letter would reach you.' He peered at Chris over the glasses, still holding the letter in his hand. 'You're a very elusive man, you know.'

'Maybe if you'll tell me what this is all about, I'll know whether I've wasted my time or not,' said Chris pointedly.

'All in good time, Mister Ranson. First I must satisfy myself on certain points and make sure that you really are the man I'm looking for.' He surveyed the other for a long moment, peering over the top of the glasses, then bent to take a paper from the lower drawer of his desk, head still cocked at an angle to look up. 'Your father, what can you tell me about him?'

Chris grinned. 'I liked him. They reckon I take after him, that's why neither of us ever went back to the family spread up north, in Cochise County. My father died more than three years ago.' There was an almost defiant tilt to his face as he went on: 'He was shot in the back by some drunken gunman in Abilene.'

'They said he was cheating at poker, wasn't that it?' murmured the other softly as he studied the papers in front of him.

'That's a lie!' In a swift, lithe movement, Chris leaned over the desk and gripped the other around the throat, fingers squeezing inexorably. Desperately, the other pulled himself back, lips working, eyes bulging from his head.

'I'm sorry . . . I — ' The other fell back in the chair as Chris released his hold on him, throat muscles working in his scrawny neck. After a moment, he sat up, rubbing this throat. 'I'm only saying what I've heard,' he muttered.

'Then you heard wrong. But you didn't ask me to come all the way to Memphis just to hear about my father.'

The other swallowed thickly. He seemed to have recovered some of his composure. Sitting forward on the edge of his chair, he riffled through the papers for a moment and then said quietly, evenly: 'You're quite right, Mister Ranson. I asked you to come here so that I might read to you the last will and testament of your grandfather, James Ellerton Ranson.'

'My grandfather!' Chris sat tall and very still in his chair, staring at the other as if unable to believe his ears.

He recalled very little of his grand-father; he had been only nine years old when he had left the vast ranch in the north and gone with his father to spend the next fourteen years south of the Texas border in the small towns of Mexico. They had been long, interesting years. He had never asked where his father had got the money which he seemed to spend so freely, not even after his mother had died that hot, sultry summer evening, with the faint rumble of thunder over the low hills in the distance, heralding the rain which would bring a little coolness to the oven-like air. Now that he came to look back on it, he remembered what the doctor had said, that she had died of some obscure coronary disease. It was as good a name for a broken heart as any.

They had buried her on the green hill outside the little town of Santa Rosita, where the deep red camellias lay like fire among the grass, and the air was warm and sweet and the only sound to disturb the deep, eternal stillness was the ringing of the Angelus from the little stone church, half a mile away. His father was now buried next to her in the same churchyard on the hill, and for three years he had been alone, drifting from one town to another on both sides of the border.

During the whole of that time, he had thought nothing of his grandfather. His only memories were of a stern and fine-featured man who ruled his ranch hands with a rod of iron, who had tried to do the same with his family; and this had been the cause of the break-up. Now, it seemed, his grandfather was dead. He leaned back in his chair. Even though his memories were dimmed by the intervening years, it still seemed impossible to believe that the old man was dead, that he no longer ruled over that vast ranch.

' . . . and to my grandson, Chris Ranson, I hereby bequeath all of my property and herd in the earnest hope that keeping it intact will make a man of him and in some way blot out the bad blood that was in his father.'

Carefully, the lawyer laid the paper down on top of the desk and glanced up at Chris, took off the spectacles and polished the lenses with his handkerchief.

'It would appear that you are the only surviving relative of the late James Ranson,' he said finally when Chris made no move to speak. 'The news has come as something of a surprise to you?'

'I scarcely remember him,' Chris rubbed his chin thoughtfully. 'He was a queer old cuss from what I do recall.' He straightened on his chair. 'So he's dead at last and the ranch belongs to me.'

'That's right.' The other regarded him keenly. 'Are you accepting it? If so, I feel it only right to warn you that you won't find things easy to handle there, and there may be danger for you.'

'Danger? What kind of danger?'

11

'All of that greed, all that crazy hate. Your grandfather was a hated man, Mister Ranson. There were more men than you could count who wanted that spread of his. He owned most of the water in the territory, he had the best grassland and the biggest herd and if that doesn't add up to a powder keg just waiting for somebody to step in and light the fuse, I don't know what does.'

'And you figure that if I ride in there and claim the ranch, I'll be ridin' right into trouble.'

'Don't you?'

'You could be right.' Chris frowned. 'Tempers can run mighty high in that part of the country. But if anybody's trying to take over the ranch then it's up to me to go back there and stop 'em.'

'You'll have the biggest fight of your life on your hands if you do,' warned the other. 'Every man in the territory will be gunning for you. From what I've heard, your grandfather was one of the

12

fastest men on the draw and nobody fancied going up against him. But now he's dead, every range wolf in the county will be setting their sights on that land and herd.'

Chris remained silent for a long time, bent forward in his chair, his arms across his knees. He seemed indrawn and sober, a lot of the assurance gone from him as he tried to absorb all of this news, felt the full weight of responsibility which had been suddenly, and unexpectedly, thrust on him. He had scarcely ever considered that one day, the ranch would be his. Most of his life had been spent in the cantinas south of the border, in a carefree existence, wanting little, his father having left him comfortably off. Life had proved to be something of a lazy, idyllic existence for him during those years. Now, quite suddenly, he had been brought up against life as it really was, with a jolt. He needed a little time in which to pause and think things over; but if what the wizened little lawyer said was true, then time was something he had little of. Already, there would be powerful and unscrupulous forces at work, scheming to take over the ranch by fair means or foul.

'Well,' said the lawyer presently, staring at him over the huge, polished desk. 'What do you intend to do? Ride on to Cochise County and take over where your grandfather left off; or take your horse and ride back south of the border, leave the place to the gun-wolves.'

Chris pressed his lips tightly together. He gave the other a bright-sharp stare.

'When my father left the ranch all those years ago, took my mother to live with him in Mexico, my grandfather disowned him, cut him off completely. True I had little to do with him then, but he must have had a reason for leavin' the place to me.'

'Evidently he thought very little of your father, even when he died,' said the other evenly. 'He mentions the bad blood in your father, hoping that you'll somehow be able to wipe that out.'

'Maybe he reckoned that I might be shot in the attempt to hold the ranch and he could get back at my father that way.' Chris spoke in a quiet, impersonal way, but there was a touch of bitterness on his face. 'If that was what he wanted, some kind of revenge beyond the grave, then this would be a good way of getting it.'

'A man would have to hate a lot to do a thing like that,' the lawyer reminded him. 'I only knew your grandfather slightly. He was never a man who made a great many friends. They either feared him or hated him and you can't base friendship on feelings like that. But he seemed to me to be a hard, though fair-minded, man. He had an iron will and he would never give in to any man. I think that was why he hated your father so much, because he had the will power to stand up against him and defy him.'

Chris got slowly to his feet, stood for a long moment looking down at the other, then said tightly. 'Reckon I'll step across to the hotel for a bite to eat. I'll come back later this afternoon when I've had time to think this whole thing over and let you know what I've decided.'

The lawyer shrugged. 'That's your privilege, Mister Ranson,' he said stiffly.

★ ★ ★

Chris crossed the dust of the street to the hotel and signed the register before climbing the squealing stairs to the room on the top floor. He pulled off his shirt and washed the trail dust off his body, filling the washbowl from the tall pitcher of water. His bones ached from the long ride; seven days on the trail, through the tall mountains and over the dry, dusty plains with a waterhole every twenty or thirty miles. Inwardly, he felt like a board that had been left out in the sun for far too long, warped and twisted and dry to the core. Up-ending the pitcher, he poured the rest of the water into the glass that stood on the small table by the bed and drank all he could hold, but he still seemed unable to slake the thirst that was deep in him, or wash all of the trail dust out of his throat. Pulling on a fresh shirt from his saddle roll, he went out into the passage outside his room, passed a couple of other rooms where the doors lay open, saw men seated there playing poker. A couple glanced up at him as he went by, curious, but not over inquisitive. A stranger in town was always likely to attract some attention, he reflected, as he made his way into the dining room, found himself a table by the wall where he could see the other diners, and ordered his meal. When it came, he ate it slowly, savouring the well cooked food which he had missed during those long days on the trail, turning things over in his mind, trying to decide what to do for the best.

Certainly he was now the last of the Ransons and the ranch itself was his heritage no matter what the reason was for his grandfather leaving it to him, clearly knowing the danger there would be. The old man would have known of the envious eyes which were cast on the spread, knew that before Chris could maintain a hold on the place, there would be bad years when the smell of gunsmoke and powder lay thick and heavy over the range and men died with a surprising suddenness. The other rich desert ranchers would try to grab off all the water and the best land for themselves and now that his grandfather was dead, now that the gunhand which had held them in check in the past was stilled in death, they would doubtless renew their efforts and let nothing stand in their way, certainly not a newcomer to the territory who, although he held claim to the ranch, would surely have to fight for it.

Finishing his meal, he sat back, found the makings of a smoke and rolled the tobacco slowly, then lit the cigarette and drew the smoke deep into his lungs. He had been weary when he had stepped down into the dining room, but the meal seemed to have acted as a stimulant and restlessness bubbled up inside him, something he found hard to control. Maybe the urges that moved a man to the wandering from one town to another were beginning to change. Maybe there came a time for every man when he wanted something more lasting and permanent, something to call his own and some place where he could sink his roots and stay for the rest of his days. Maybe a man would even be prepared to fight for such a thing, to fight and to kill if that were the only way he could hold it.

He returned to the livery stable to check on his horse, then made his way slowly to the lawyer's office. The other gave him a brief nod as he entered, motioned to him to be seated.

'Had time to think this over?' he asked.

'I reckon so,' Chris nodded. 'I've decided to ride up into Cochise County and take over the ranch.'

The lawyer gave him a slow look of surprise, as if this had not been the answer he had been expecting. He said: 'You know your own mind better than anybody, I suppose. I only hope that you've made the right, and wise, decision.'

'I guess so. I reckon it's the only decision I can make in the circumstances.' He had surveyed all of the other possibilities during the minutes he had sat over his meal at the hotel, had turned them carefully in his mind while musing through the pale haze of smoke from his cigarette. True, the future was something that had no promise of anything definite for him other than perhaps an uncertain and maybe impecunious hardship. Danger he expected, but he was still far from being free of the nagging uncertainty and that troubled him more than he dared admit, even to himself. As he sat there in that dusty, drab office, he wondered what plans might be being laid against him, even at that moment, for he did not doubt that word of this would already have reached the men who would be waiting to kill him.

He thought about that a lot more throughout the evening, wondering again if he had done the right thing but each time that doubts assailed him, the thought came to him that his grandfather, no matter what else might have been said against him, had made the vast ranch himself, had built it with his own two hands in the hard, old days just before the Civil War, had made it into what it was. He had made it not only for himself, but for the Ranson family so that the name might come to mean something in that part of the territory. He had made this small empire, proclaimed himself the head of it; and now it was up to him to carry on the name.

★ ★ ★

Bob Dunson dragged his spurs over the yard of the ranch, raking up little snakeheads of dust under his feet. At the porch, he hesitated for a moment, turned to throw a quick glance about him, at the horses moving in the corral and the cattle which were clustered high up on the brow of the hills in the distance. Then he pushed open the door with the flat of his hand and strode inside.

Taking off his hat, he looked about him with wary eyes, swung swiftly as the door opened and Matt Wilder stepped into the room. The other brought his glance to Dunson and looked at him for a thoughtful moment. 'You've been a long time,' he said, thinly, 'what did you find out in Memphis?'

'Jest what you figgered,' muttered the other. He sank down into the nearby chair as the other poured a drink into a glass and held it out to him. 'That lawyer fella managed to locate old man Ranson's grandson. They say he was way down in Mexico, south of the border. Made quite a name for himself down there.'

Wilder's brows went up a little. 'What sort of a name'?' he queried.

'Not as a gunman, that's a fact,' grinned the other. 'I'd guess you'd call him a gambler like his father. Ain't surprised the old man wanted nothing much to do with either of 'em.'

'So it shouldn't be too difficult to get rid of him, one way or another,' murmured the other musingly. He rubbed a hand down his face.

Dunson watched the other steadily over the rim of his glass, trying to guess at the thoughts now in the other's mind. 'You figuring on stopping him before he gets here? Reckon that would be the simplest way of makin' sure.'

'The simplest way, maybe, but not the best way,' countered the other, his face suddenly hard as he turned the possibilities over in his mind. 'This has got to look like an accident. You know as well as I do, that there are still a lot of folk in this territory who thought a lot of old man Ranson. They'll stick by his grandson if he's anythin' like the old man. From what you say, that ain't likely, but we have to play this hand carefully.'

'Better be sure that you don't wait too long before makin' your play,' muttered Dunson. He finished his drink, laid the empty glass on the table. 'There are more than you with eyes on the Ranson spread. If they make their play first, you may find that you're squeezed out.'

'You think I don't know that. I know all about Webber and Diego. I can call twice as many men to my back as they can between them — and they know that. If they step out of line as far as this deal is concerned, they'll be shot to pieces and they'll lose everything they have now.'

'You want me to keep an eye open along the trail? He was still in Memphis when I pulled out, but I reckon if he left the next mornin' he can't be more than a day's ride behind me.'

Wilder nodded tersely. 'Do that,' he

ordered. 'Let me know the minute he rides into town. I figure he may head there for a word with Sheriff Maxwell before he moves on to the ranch.'

★   ★   ★

It was late morning before Chris Ranson reached the long line of timber which reared up on the slopes of the low hills. Down below him lay Cochise County and the vast Ranson spread, and a few moments later, he came upon the trail that wound down through the trees, then through the narrow ravine, at the lower end of which the trail widened, moved across a river and then vanished into the rocks on the far side. He halted his mount, sat tall in the saddle, his eyes fixed ahead, but seeing little, lips tightly compressed. Depression chilled his spirit a little as he struggled with his thoughts.

Finishing his smoke, he went on, crossed a bare bench of ground that opened out like a scar among the trees.

There were a few blackened stumps on the edge of the open stretch and it was obvious that fire had destroyed the undergrowth here at some time in the past, possibly during the war, for this was part of the land which had been fought over during the long battle of the Wilderness. Half an hour onward, he came across a narrow footbridge that stretched over a deep gorge with a narrow, swift-running stream at the bottom of it.

He glanced at the creek, running fast and white, creaming with foam where the water splashed and raced among the sharp-pointed boulders which thrust up from the rocky bed, then put his mount to the bridge, listening to the hollowness of its hoofbeats on the wood. Somewhere close by the bridge, but still out of sight, he was able to pick out the sound of the falls which had produced this creek, dropping with a steady thunder down the side of the rock face. The mist from the falls lay in the air with a thin dampness that touched his face and neck and brought a quiet coolness to everything. Even the vegetation here seemed to grow more densely and lushly than anywhere else along the trail.

He turned a sharp corner in the trail just beyond the far end of the bridge and came suddenly on the bare patch which had been cleared away at the very foot of the mountain wall. Here, there was a wooden shack, little more than a lean-to, with the far wall set simply against the bare rock. The contrast between the grey, weathered rock and the tall green-topped pines that marched away in every direction from the hut, was tremendous, almost breath-taking. A couple of mangy dogs came scuffing towards him, stood on top of a small knoll, sniffing the air at him, their tails between their legs.

Chris sat quite still as a man moved into sight from around the side of the cabin, a rifle held loosely in his right hand. He had a thin, stretched face, with wrinkles showing around the eyes and mouth, a face from which it was impossible to tell if he was old or young. Chris reckoned he was about six feet in height, but the slimness of his build made him seem even taller.

For a long moment, the other stared at him through narrowed eyes, suspicious of him. The two dogs came snarling forward, but still keeping a safe distance, as if they too were unsure of him.

'You lookin' for somethin', stranger, or jest ridin'?' asked the other after a long pause.

'I'm lookin' for the Ranson place,' said Chris softly. He eyed the rifle which the other still held in his hand. The man stared at him for a few moments longer and then lowered the hand that held the gun. 'Still quite a ways from here,' he said harshly. 'Reckon you won't make it before evenin'. You look like you've been ridin' for quite a spell. Get down and come inside.'

Gratefully, Chris climbed from the

saddle, let the horse go free. There was no place it could wander here and he doubted if it would make the return journey over the narrow bridge above the deep, steep-sided canyon.

'You got any reason for lookin' for the Ranson spread?' grunted the other as he bent his head and led the way inside the shack.

'Some,' said Chris casually. 'I'm Chris Ranson. I got word a couple of days ago that my grandfather was dead and the place had been left to me.'

The other stolidly accepted the information, gave a brief nod of his head as he laid his glance on Chris, the look like the edge of a knife, motionless but ready to cut. Chris guessed he was one of the lonesome sort, a man who came out to this wild wilderness to be away from other men, perhaps preferring the company of the dogs to that of his fellow men.

'So you're Jim Ranson's grandson,' he said. 'Well, I reckon you know what you're up against. There's a mighty lot of men who'd like to get their hands on that spread.'

'So I've been told. You know anythin' about 'em?'

'Some.' The other motioned him to the table, spread with food. 'Jest because I live up here, don't mean that I know nothin' of what goes on down in the valley. Reckon I know more'n most folk. Matt Wilder tried to get the ranch some years ago, but your grandfather wouldn't sell. Wilder's ranch butts on to the Ranson place and he needs more water than he's got. Any man other than Jim Ranson would have been run out of the territory once Wilder started. But your grandfather stood up to him, forced him to pull in his horns like a salted snail.' The bushy brows went up in an expression of mute interrogation. 'You figger that you're the same kind of man, that you can stand up to men like Wilder or Diego?'

His gaze had dropped to the belt around Chris's waist. 'See you ain't carryin' guns. A man needs guns if he's to stay alive around these parts, specially with men like Diego and Wilder gunnin' for him.'

'No reason for anybody to know who I am just yet.'

The other shook his head as he seated himself at the other side of the table. 'You're a danged fool if you believe that. Wilder will know that you're ridin' in already. He'll have had one of his men, probably Dunson, watchin' for you.' The bright, bird-like stare fixed on Chris again. 'Where'd you get the news about the ranch?'

'Memphis. The lawyer there sent word across the border to Santa Rosita.'

'Then I figure you can bet your bottom dollar that Dunson would be there, in Memphis. Reckon that must've been him I saw ridin' hell for leather yesterday along the valley trail.'

Chris gave him a tight look. 'You seem to have got your fingers on a lot of things in these parts for all that you live so far off the beaten track.'

'A stranger ridin' into town will be

suspected, particularly now that old man Ranson is dead. They'll know that sooner or later, you'd come ridin' in to claim the ranch. You couldn't fool them even if you tried.'

'Then you figure I'm a fool.' Chris looked directly at the rangy man.

The other shrugged. 'Either that, or there's a heap more to you than I can see right now. I know the sort of man that your grandfather was, but whether you can stand in his shoes or not, I'm not sure.'

'Were you a friend of my grandfather's?'

The other chewed thoughtfully on a mouthful of food for a long moment as if turning that question over in his mind. He said finally: 'Reckon your grandfather had no friends. But he was a straight, honest man and that's why a lot of the folk here respected him. They knew that he'd back 'em in any fight that came between them and men like Wilder and Diego. So long as he was around, they felt safe. Now he's dead, they're not sure of themselves any longer. They know that it's only a matter of time before Wilder starts to move in on them, to take over their spreads.'

'And the men on the ranch,' asked Chris quietly. 'You know anythin' about them? Whether they'll stay and take orders from me, or whether they'll ride on over the hill?'

'Reckon that's up to you. If you're a hard man like your grandfather, then they'll follow you clear to Hell and back. But if not, if you're soft, then they'll pull out and leave you, maybe even go over to the other side.'

Chris was silent for a long moment, staring straight ahead of him. Then he stirred as if aware of the other's presence in the room. 'Thanks for lettin' me know how things are,' he said quietly. 'And thanks for the grub. Maybe I can do the same for you sometime.'

'Mebbe,' acknowledged the other meaningly. 'If you live that long. There's a mighty powerful group against you. But they won't kill you straight out, they'll want to make it look like an accident. That is, until you've shown yourself in your true colours. If you're soft, then nobody is goin' to mind if you're dead or alive, but if you make a stand against Diego and Wilder, you'll have the same kind of respect from the small ranchers as he got.'

'And the law in the territory?'

'You mean Sheriff Maxwell? He's in cahoots with Wilder. Trust him and you're as good as dead.' He looked at Chris with a moment's penetrating attention. 'I don't quite know about you.'

'For you,' said Chris, calmly dismissing the statement, 'I guess it doesn't matter.'

'Mebbe not. This is your business, I reckon. But if you do try to go for Wilder, you'll have to break through a host of gunslingers to get at him.'

Later that evening, Chris left the cabin, picked up his horse and made a wide circle through the timber before striking the trail a couple of miles further down the mountainside. The sun was dipping low towards the western horizon on his left and his shadow grew long and huge on the ground beside him as he rode. The main stage trail lay far below him, down in the valley and he could occasionally make it out through gaps in the trees, a scar of grey against the overall greenness. The sun flamed in a vast haze of red and scarlet as it touched the rim of the world, touching the tops of the tall hills with flame, leaving the floor of the deep valley in hazy shadow. Far below him, he could make out the small township that stood at the junction of the trails from the hills. In the length of time since he had left the small shack to the moment he rode out of the timber belt and came upon the open stretches of rock and huge up-thrusting boulders where the narrow mountain trail dipped to the valley, no rider moved along the wide stage trail. The very stillness of the hills spoke its own voice of tension. It was as if the world was waiting tensely for something to happen, something which had been hanging fire for some time now, but was now about to break. It was the feeling he had whenever a storm lay close to the horizon, with the oven-heat and the stillness hanging like a mighty pressure over everything.

He paused for a long moment at the head of the descending trail, sitting loose and relaxed in the saddle. But it was only his body that was relaxed, muscles loosened a little. His mind was still alert and tensed. He had learned a lot from that man back there in the cabin against the mountainside. What he had learned had not helped to ease the tension in his mind. The thought of this man Matt Wilder, and the others, waiting to move in and grab the ranch, knowing of his coming, disturbed him anew. It was a signal of things to come, of the problems and dangers that faced him in this wide, stretching valley which the deep, quiet hills seemed to heed.

He was half a mile down the trail, his horse picking its way forward with care among the treacherous boulders that lay strewn along the narrow, winding trail, when he heard the first faint whispers of sound in the distance. The sun had gone down behind the western horizon and the redness in the sky had given way to the deep, cool blue and indigo and he reined his mount, listening to the tattoo of sound as the other rider came forward, pushing his mount at a punishing pace. He moved his horse into the shadows of the rocks, looked down at the stage trail, now less than half a mile below him, trying to pick out the shape of the rider.

Seconds later, horse and rider came into view, moving swiftly in a cloud of churned-up dust along the lower trail. It was too dark and the other too far away for Chris to be able to make out his features and the rider's steady echo faded swiftly into the night, presently dying into silence.

By the time he approached the

outskirts of the town the starlight laid a faint trembling glow over the trail and there was still the smell of dust in the air, indicating that men were travelling these trails. He felt a sense of uneasiness as he rode into the wide street, eyes alert, watchful for trouble. Tying up the horse in front of the first saloon he came to, he went inside. Six men were clustered around a table in one corner where a poker game was in progress and there were others at more tables, with a couple standing against the bar. As he went over to the bar, all six men playing poker stopped their game and eyed him with a curious steadfastness, then went back to their play as they saw him eyeing them through the mirror at the rear of the long bar.

Resting his elbows on the bar, Chris glanced at the bartender. The other moved slowly in his direction, stood stolidly in front of him, waiting.

'Where can a man eat in this town?' Chris asked.

'You can either get a meal over at the hotel, or take your luck with anything we've got here,' said the man softly.

'I'll take a chance with what you've got,' Chris said. He picked up the glass and bottle which the other had brought over with him and poured himself a drink, only half filling the glass. He held the drink between his fingers for a long moment, staring down at it while the barkeep watched him for a moment with no expression on his round, red face, then moved away, disappearing into the room at the back of the bar.

Drinking, Chris watched the men at his back through the mirror. One or two of them were still glancing almost furtively in his direction, sure that he was keeping them under surveillance, but wondering about him. Maybe a stranger in town was sufficiently rare to evoke such curiosity, he thought inwardly, but then on the other hand, it might be that this man Wilder had passed word along to his cronies in town to keep their eyes open for any stranger riding in, particularly if he looked as if he had been on the trail for some time.

Ten minutes later, the bartender came back, ran a wet cloth over the bar, then said quietly: 'Find yourself a table, friend, and I'll bring your meal across to you. Take the bottle along with you.'

Chris nodded, gripped the bottle by the neck and carried it to one of the empty tables, standing a little apart from those which were occupied. None of the men in the room had stirred since he had come in. Then, one of them scraped back his chair, got heavily to his feet, and walked across to his table, stood in front of it for a long moment, looking down at him, waiting for the invitation to sit down.

It was some time in coming. Chris was unsure how he would be able to tell those men who had been on speaking terms with his grandfather from those who wanted him dead. There was the feel of danger all about him. He guessed this town was likely to be the same as a score of others he had known, full of dodgers, men running from something, be it the law or others of their kind seeking revenge, and probably the best trade this saloon got was from men such as these.

'Sit down, friend,' he said at last, waving a hand towards the chair opposite him. He pushed the bottle towards the other, eyed him closely. 'You look like a man who has something on his mind.'

'Just curious,' said the other openly. 'You figuring on staying around these parts or just ridin' through?'

'Depends a lot on what I find here,' said Chris easily. His gaze locked with the other's, held fast. 'Might be I'd find myself a spread and settle down.'

'Ain't no land here for the buyin',' grunted the other. 'Most of the smaller ranchers are movin' out, headin' back east.'

Chris raised his brows as if in surprise. 'Could be I'd be able to pick up one of their spreads cheap,' he remarked.

The other shook his head emphatically. 'Not a chance. Either Matt Wilder or Diego will get 'em. Nobody stays long in these parts.'

'Did hear there was a big ranch a couple of miles out of town, to the north.'

'You mean the Ranson place?' The other grinned. 'Mister, if you're figgerin' on tryin' to get a hold of that spread, better forget about it right now.'

'Any reason why?' Chris spoke deliberately, with a casualness that was far from casual.

The other did not seem to have noticed. His smile was a tight-lipped thing that merely deepened the lines around the corners of his mouth and eyes. 'Half a dozen reasons, and all good ones,' he said shortly. 'Old man Ranson died a few weeks ago. Nobody knows what's going to happen as far as the spread is concerned, but both Wilder and Diego and maybe half a dozen more of the big men are after it, and you can be sure one of 'em will get it, even though there'll be gunplay before it's finally settled.'

'That,' said Chris at long length, 'is open to question.' He turned as the bartender came over with the meal, setting in front of him fried potatoes, beans and bacon and a mug of hot, black coffee.

'Well,' murmured the other, 'they do say there's a grandson somewhere, but he ain't lived here for close on twelve or thirteen years. From what I've heard tell, he's a dude, spends all of his time living it up in the cantinas south of the Texas border — and that's a mighty long way from Cochise County.'

Chris finished the rest of his meal in silence, acutely aware of the other's glance, but giving no sign of it. Lighting a smoke, he sipped the hot coffee, felt it burn the back of his throat on the way down. 'This seems to be one hell of a place,' he said softly, blowing the smoke into the air in front of his face.

'It is now,' agreed the other. 'While old man Ranson was alive, there was some kind of law and order about the place. Now that he's dead, that's all gone by the board. Wilder and Diego are runnin' things their way and Sheriff Maxwell is carrying out their orders.'

'A crooked sheriff in town and the beginnings of a full-scale range war out on the prairie,' mused Chris softly. 'Seems I've ridden into trouble here.'

'Better get your horse and ride out tomorrow,' advised the other. He poured a drink from the bottle, gulped it down. 'This is no place for anybody who has no part in this quarrel.'

Chris sat for several moments in his chair, savouring the smoke. 'I'll think on what you've said,' he muttered, getting to his feet.

He tossed a couple of coins on to the bar, then walked out, across to the hotel.

2

Marked for Violence

Chris walked through the small lobby of the hotel, waking the man who lay sprawled in the chair behind the desk, his mouth open, snoring loudly. The man opened his red-rimmed eyes, glanced up, made to close them again, then sat up straight and sudden in his chair before finally scrambling to his feet.

'You got a room?' Chris asked tersely. He still felt jumpy inside and spoke more sharply to the other than he had intended.

'Sure, plenty of room,' grunted the other. He rubbed the back of his hand over his mouth. 'How long are you figuring on stayin'?'

'A couple of days.' Chris turned the register, signed his name with a flourish, then swung it back to face the other. He saw the clerk glance down at the name, saw his gaze flick away without any recognition in it, then suddenly swing back as the significance of what he saw went home. He looked up at Chris with his jaw hanging slackly open. 'Ranson!' he said thinly, as if unable to believe his eyes. 'Say, you ain't no relative of old Jim Ranson who died a couple of weeks ago, are you?'

Chris nodded slowly, his gaze holding the other's. 'I'm his grandson,' he said evenly, casually.

'Well, I'd never have guessed it,' murmured the other. He was wide awake now, moved around the edge of the desk, looking along the lobby for any luggage the other might have brought with him. Disappointed at seeing nothing, he turned. 'This all you have?' he asked, nodding his head towards the saddle roll on the floor behind the desk.

'That's right. Now about that bed, old-timer. I've been more'n two days on the trail and I could do with a good night's sleep.'

'Sure, sure.' The other moved quickly around the edge of the desk, swept a key from the wooden rack on the wall and handed it over to him. 'First floor, at the far end of the passage,' he said quickly. 'If you want anythin' before mornin', just holler. I'm here all night.'

'I'll remember that,' Chris nodded, picked up the saddle roll, slung it over his shoulder and made his way up the creaking stairway, along the narrow corridor on the first floor and opened the door of the room at the end, locking the door behind him. It was cool inside the room and he opened the window a little, peering down on to the street below the hotel. From the window, with no light on in the room at his back, he could see everything that went on down there, hear everything. He had been standing there for less than ten seconds when he heard the faint sound of the hotel doors being opened. Pulling himself back from the window, pressing his body tightly against the wall to one side, he peered down, taking care not to be seen by anyone in the street below.

The dark figure came creeping out of the hotel door almost immediately below him, moved out cautiously into the middle of the dark street and paused there for a long moment, staring furtively about him, then lifting his head to peer up at the window of Chris's room. Finally, he was satisfied that no one was watching him and moved off, across the street, on to the boardwalk on the far side, his body alternately hidden in darkness and alternately hazed by the yellow light from the windows of the buildings on the other side of the street. But by that time, Chris had seen enough to know who it was. There had been no mistaking the small figure of the desk clerk.

Now where would he be running to at that time of night? Chris wondered tightly. Seemed there would be only one answer to that. He was the only man in town who knew who he was and now he was hot-footing it out of town to pass on the news, either to Wilder, Diego, or perhaps Sheriff Maxwell.

He kept the door of his room locked as he went back and stretched himself out on the long, low bed. There was the deep weariness of the long ride along the trail in every fibre and muscle of his body, an ache that had been with him now for many days, something he could neither rid himself of nor forget. A hat for a pillow and the hard, stony ground for his bed; and often no fire to keep him warm through the long, cold, starlit nights when the blackness had crowded in from the far horizons of a vast world and the stillness had been heightened and sharpened by the thousands of pinpoints of brilliant light in the heavens. It had been a deep and bitter loneliness which he had known out there on the trail. The kind of loneliness that had been known by man long before he had become civilised, when he had looked out on the moon and the bright constellations and wondered what it had all meant; a fear-filled, frightening loneliness that had somehow left its mark on him, left him with something he had not known before.

In spite of the deep-seated uneasiness in him, Chris Ranson slept, surrendering to the weariness in his body and mind. When he woke, the pale grey light of an early dawn filtered through the windows and there was the breathless hush that came with it in these frontier towns. A horse whinnied softly from somewhere along the street, but that was the only sound that broke the deep silence. He lay for a moment with his hands clasped behind his neck, staring up at the ceiling, remembering everything that had happened the previous day; the warning he had been given by the man in the saloon; a man who had not known who he was — and the way in which the desk clerk had slipped out of the hotel once he figured that Chris was safely asleep in his room.

By now, everybody who mattered

would know that Jim Ranson's grandson had come riding into town, that he had put up for the night at the hotel. Was there a plan being laid against him at that moment, while he lay there doing nothing? The thought stirred him into action. Swinging his legs to the floor, he washed in the basin at the window, listening to the other, faint sounds outside in the street. The town was shaking itself awake, ready for another hot day.

Downstairs, he went into the dining room for an early breakfast. The man behind the desk in the lobby was not the same one who had been there the night before and he guessed that the other had gone off duty. He found a table, waited for the meal to come, then ate ravenously. He had missed good cooking all the time he had been on the trail and he meant to make up for it while he had the chance.

He was on the point of getting up after finishing the meal when he noticed the tall man who came into the diner,

51

standing looking about him for a moment, before turning and coming over to his table. The other was a broad-shouldered, heavy-set man, going to fat now, with broad jowls and thick lips. He paused in front of Chris's table.

'Mister Ranson?' he said harshly.

Chris glanced up, then waved the other towards the empty chair. 'That's my name,' he said easily. He noticed the silver star pinned on the other's shirt, the weight of it pulling the thin material away from the other's vest. 'Won't you sit down, Sheriff. I suppose the desk clerk told you I was here last night.'

The other's eyes narrowed and for a moment there was a dangerous look on his face, then he seemed to pull himself together, the broad lips opened in a wide grin, the right hand dropped from the neighbourhood of his gun butt and he lowered himself slowly into the chair.

'All right, Mister Ranson,' he said quietly. 'Seems you know a lot more than I had given you credit for. So the clerk did happen to mention to me that you'd registered here. But that was only because I'd asked him to do so. I heard that you might be ridin' into town sometime. We figured that you'd get word about your grandfather dying and you'd be ridin' in to take over the ranch and I reckoned it was kind of important that I had the chance to get a word with you before you rode out to the ranch.'

'You got somethin' on your mind, Sheriff?' asked Chris innocently.

'Well, let's say there may be trouble if things get out of hand,' said the other, lips pursed a little. 'And as the sheriff here it's my job to see that there ain't no real trouble.'

Chris leaned back in his chair, eyeing the other closely. 'Sheriff Maxwell,' he said softly. 'All I came here for was to take over where my grandfather left off. I fail to see why that should cause any trouble for anybody.'

'Well, now, let's not rush into this before we know all the facts,' said the other soothingly. 'Things are a little more complicated than that. Your grandfather was a strong man, fast with a gun. Nobody fancied trying to take anythin' from him, land or water, or even cattle. There was some rustlin' from the other spreads, but never from his. He had a way of exactin' retribution whenever it was needed, that usually deterred anybody from tryin' it with him. But he's dead now and I'm wonderin' if you're the right man to take over in his shoes. I ought to warn you here and now that there are powerful men such as Matt Wilder who want to buy that spread. They'll pay good money for it and if any of 'em approaches you with a proposition, then I'd pay it real serious consideration. They'll offer you a fair price and you'll be able to ride back to where you came from a very rich man. Why stay here and stick your neck out for nothin' when you could have all that?'

'Then I take it that you're advisin' me to sell out if I get an offer for the spread and the ranch?' Chris looked at him, open-eyed.

'That's right. Make things easier all round.' The other smiled, obviously well pleased with himself. 'I always say there's a peaceable way to do everythin' if you only take the trouble to look for it.'

'And supposin' that I refuse to sell?' Chris looked the other squarely in the eye. 'Supposin' I figure on takin' over the ranch and runnin' it as my grandfather did?'

The other's lips tightened suddenly. His face grew a mite ugly. 'Then you'd find yourself in more trouble than you've ever dreamed of,' he stated flatly. 'And I wouldn't be able to answer for the consequences.'

'You tryin' to say that if any of these men, Wilder, or Diego, tried to grab that land from me, you'd stand by and do nothin'? I thought you were the law in these parts.'

'I'm the law as far as this town is concerned,' corrected the other stiffly. 'There ain't no law out yonder on the prairie. The ranchers make their own law and until the Rangers move in, there's nothin' I could do.'

Chris smiled thinly. He said: 'You seem to have made your position in this matter quite clear, Sheriff.' A glinting expression showed on his face. 'I reckon it's only fair I do the same. I'll be ridin' out to the ranch tomorrow and takin' it over. There'll be no question of sellin' it, to Wilder or anybody else.'

'That your last word, Ranson?' said the sheriff, pushing himself stiffly to his feet. There was a faint flush high in his cheeks, and his eyes were sharp-bright under lowered brows.

'That's right,' Chris nodded. 'You found that you couldn't run my grandfather out of the territory when he stood up against tyranny and you'll find the same with me.'

'I doubt it,' answered the sheriff. 'Your kind never likes to shoot it out with a man used to handling a fast gun. D'you think we know nothin' about you? We know of the way you used to live down in Mexico, we know the kind of man your father was and they always say: like father, like son. In this case, I'm goshdarned sure that it's true.'

'Then you guess wrong,' said Chris. He did not allow any of the deep, bitter, anger to show in his face. Only the tight-knuckled grip of his hands on the edge of the table showed anything of the emotions in him.

The sharp glitter of tight, angry amusement died out of Sheriff Maxwell's face. He got to his feet, stood for a moment with his gaze held tight on the other man's features as though trying to read what lay deep beneath that hard, inscrutable expression. Then he said in a strained voice: 'Don't try to fight these men, because you just can't do it. Only man who ever could stand up to 'em and make 'em back down, has just died. You're not the kind of man to step into his shoes and I reckon you know it.'

It was the waiter who broke the tension by coming forward until he

57

stood beside the sheriff. 'You want breakfast here, Sheriff?' he asked quietly.

The other shook his head, his face suffused with a dark anger. 'No thanks, I never eat before noon.' Turning sharply on his heel, he stalked out of the dining room. A moment later, Chris heard the front door of the hotel slam as the other left and he caught a brief, fragmentary glimpse of him walking swiftly across the street, shadow long beside him as the sun came up over the hills which lay to the east.

The waiter stood beside the table, glanced down at Chris. 'Seems you set his back up, rubbed him the wrong way, mister,' he said softly. 'He can be a bad man to fall foul of, if you get my meaning.'

'I get it,' Chris nodded. He crushed out his smoke, pushed back his chair and made his way up to his room.

★   ★   ★

When he went down into the street an hour later, the sun was well up and the heat lay thick and heavy in the air. Not a breath of wind stirred the dust on the wide street and there were few people about. He checked at the livery stable, made sure that his horse had everything it needed. As he was coming out from the rear, the groom stepped out of the shadows and came forward, eyeing him curiously.

'You the fella who just rode in from Memphis last night?' he asked softly, head cocked a little on one side, his eyes bright like those of a magpie.

'That's right,' Chris nodded, paused, stood with his shoulders resting against the thick, wooden upright.

'There's some talk about town that you're Jim Ranson's grandson.' The other had a sly humour on his face and a bright and beady wisdom in his eyes. Here, reflected Chris, was a man who would see everything that went on in town, would evidently know everything, and he wouldn't be likely to have lined up with anyone on either side of the feuding parties.

'And if it's true?' countered Chris. He watched the old fellow and wondered how much he knew about him, whether he would talk, and if he did, how much of it would be factual truth.

'Then I reckon you're either a brave man or a goshdarned fool.' He squinted up at Chris's face in the slanting beams of sunlight that filtered through a wide window in the low, slanting roof of the building. 'You don't look like a fool to me.'

'You know if there were any men my grandfather trusted?' asked Chris tautly.

'You mean apart from those who worked for him on the ranch?' The other rubbed a horny hand over his chin, the stubble rasping under the hard flesh. 'I reckon there's Doc Fordham and Frank Jargens — he owns the local newspaper. You may find Jargens reluctant to help. Now that Jim Ranson's dead, Wilder will have warned him of the consequences if he prints anythin' against him.'

'It figures,' nodded Chris. 'For a lot of reasons. But I reckon I might pay a call on this Doctor Fordham.'

'Me,' said the groom, 'I'm so old that nobody cares a hoot about me. But I know a lot more'n I ever tell. Reckon if I told all that I knew, I'd no longer be an old man, I'd be a dead one.' He threw a quick, meaningful glance at Chris's waist, then lifted his eyes back to the other's face. 'Notice you ain't totin' any guns,' he said, and there was a hopeful curiosity in his tone, his head bent forward a little, clearly waiting for an answer.

'Haven't found any need to carry 'em so far.' Chris rolled a smoke, firmed it between his fingers, then lit it, scraping the sulphur match down the side of the wall beside him. From where he stood, it was just possible to see the street for perhaps thirty yards, but he could not be seen himself unless someone out there was deliberately looking for him and he didn't think that likely at the moment. But the smoke provided him with an excuse for standing there apparently doing nothing and he knew, inwardly, that he needed the answers to one hell of a lot of questions before he would feel himself to be on sure ground in this territory.

There was no doubt that his grandfather had made himself a whole heap of enemies here and it was essential that he should be able to recognise them before he went much further. There were sure to be some folk here who might talk to him, provided he got to them before Matt Wilder, or Diego, did. He could guess at the means these men would use to persuade such people not to talk to him. And as far as the folk in this part of the county were concerned, he was an unknown quantity and no man in his right mind would be willing to risk his life for someone like that.

'Just where do I find Doc Fordham?' he asked at length, dropping the glowing butt of his cigarette on to the stone floor and crushing it out carefully under his heel.

The other stepped forward, pointed along the street. 'Fifty yards along on the other side,' he grunted. 'You goin' to stay here, take over the ranch?'

'It looks that way,' Chris said quietly. There was something in his voice which made the other look up at him in mild surprise. Then the oldster nodded. 'Could be that you are a chip off the old block at that,' he murmured. 'Sure, but I reckon there'll be hell let loose if you are.'

Chris made to say something further, then changed his mind and swung out of the livery stables, out on to the boardwalk, ducking his head under one of the wooden overhangs, glancing right and left at the folk who moved past him. A minute later, he stood in front of the doctor's office, an unpretentious place, with very little to mark it out from any of the other buildings on either side of it. He rapped loudly on the door, waited until he heard the sound of footsteps approaching. There was the rattle of a chain and a moment later, the door opened and a tall, white-haired man stood in the opening, peering out at him. Chris had an impression of a kindly, lined face, filled with the character of the man. He guessed instantly that here was a man who would not back down easily, nor run from what he considered to be right.

'Doctor Fordham?' he asked quietly.

The other gave a quick nod, his brow furrowed in thought as he tried to place this stranger. 'That is my name,' he answered, 'but I'm afraid that I — '

'I'm Chris Ranson.' He saw the sudden gust of expression that came over the older man's face, saw the look which the name evoked in the man's grey eyes. Then Fordham had reached out, caught him by the arm, pulling him inside his office, after throwing a quick glance up and down the street. The door was shut behind him, the chain put back into place. Then the other was ushering him along a narrow passage into the room at the back of the building. Chris caught a glimpse of a larger room through an open door which he took to be the surgery.

'Somehow, I never figured that you'd come here,' muttered the other, as he motioned Chris to a chair. 'I heard that you were somewhere in Texas, or maybe even south of there, over the border. But I never thought for one moment that you would come riding back to claim the ranch. I reckoned it would go to the man who proved himself top dog in these parts, who killed all other opposition and stepped in to take the spoils.'

Chris forced a quick, tight grin. 'It seems that I've made quite a lot of people change their plans,' he said simply. He lowered himself gratefully into the chair, watched the other as the doctor went over to a small, wall cupboard and took out a bottle and two glasses which he set down on the nearby table.

'How did you know to come to me?' asked the other, as he poured the drinks.

'I got to talking with the groom down at the livery stable and he mentioned your name when I asked who was likely to have been my grandfather's friends.'

'Did he mention anyone else?' The other handed Chris the glass, sank down into the chair opposite him.

'The owner of the local newspaper,' said Chris, sipping the whisky.

'Frank Jargens,' Fordham nodded his head slowly. 'He was your grandfather's friend, that's very true. But I'm not so sure of him now. Matt Wilder was in the office yesterday, talking very confidentially with him. I've no idea what they were talking about, but you can be sure Wilder knows you're here in town and he'll be scheming how to get rid of you without making it look too darned obvious.'

'Just what sort of a man is Wilder?' Chris felt the whiskey burning in his stomach.

'Rotten, all the way through,' declared the other without hesitation. 'I've known him since he came here from somewhere back east. That was more'n fifteen years ago. Bought himself a small spread with money he said he got during the war. Then he started lending out to the small ranchers in these parts, taking over mortgages on their spreads. When they failed to meet the deadline with cash on the nail, he simply went in and took over. There was nothin' they could do to stop him. Everything was quite legal and above board.'

'That sounds like the usual thing,' nodded Chris. He held out his glass at a nod from the other, as Fordham filled it for him. 'And in time, he became one of the most powerful men in these parts.'

'That's it,' acknowledged the other. He gazed at Chris over the rim of his glass. 'Only man he couldn't make back down was Jim Ranson. He tried, but your grandfather took a score of his men and rode out to Wilder's place and shot up several of his boys. Since that time, there was a kind of uneasy truce between the two. Now that your grandfather is dead, Wilder has seen his chance and he means to move in and take over as fast as he can.'

'And now that I've turned up it complicates matters a little for him.'

'It complicates matters a whole lot. This place is a powder keg and it only needs one little spark to set off the fuse, and once that is lit, nothin' is going to put it out until the whole lot goes up in a full-scale range war.'

'A lot of folk have told me I ought to ride back to Mexico and forget about the ranch. Sheriff Maxwell suggested I should accept the offer which he feels sure that Wilder is going to make, then leave this territory. So far, nobody thinks it would be a good thing for me to ride in and take the ranch.'

Doc Fordham looked at him searchingly for a long moment. Then he scratched his lean jaw thoughtfully. 'I'd like to be able to tell you that,' he said softly. 'But even if I did, I don't know whether it would be the best thing to do. It needs a man as good as, or better, than your grandfather to tame this country. A man has to be quick and sure on the draw — and I notice you got no guns.'

'Might be that I figure there's another way to keep the ranch without havin' to resort to gunplay,' said Chris soberly.

The other shook his head emphatically. 'There's no other way here, believe me,' he murmured fervently. 'I know these men. I've seen them grow from nothing to what they are now. They only did that by the law of the gun and they know that's the only way they can stay as they are. They'll fight tooth and nail, not only to keep what they've got, but to get hold of more.'

'I came all the way from Santa Rosita to claim this ranch and I don't aim to back down now,' said Chris tightly.

'You'll stay and fight men like Wilder, men with more than sixty hired gunslingers at their back, ready to ride in and grab what they can at a moment's notice.'

'That's right.'

'Well, I wish you wouldn't, but I know that you will,' said Fordham. Again, the long, slender-fingered hand rubbed over his jaw.

★ ★ ★

'It's a safe bet that Ranson will stay in town until he's sure of himself,' opined Dunson sombrely, 'and we can ride in there any time and take him.'

Wilder said nothing for a long moment, turning the news over in his mind. It had come as no surprise to him to hear from Maxwell that Ranson had put up at the hotel in town, nor that he had been asking a lot of questions around the place.

'You want me to arrest him on some charge or other?' put in the sheriff, standing by the windows in the front parlour of the Wilder ranch house.

'If we try to frame some charge

70

against him and put him in jail, just what do we achieve?' frowned Wilder. He stirred himself in his chair. 'Very little. We'd have to fix it so that we could string him up from the nearest tree and that wouldn't be easy, not with everybody in town probably knowing who he is by now. There are still too many folk there who remember Jim Ranson and they'll back his grandson if we try that.'

'Better if we have the showdown right here and now,' muttered Dunson thinly. He touched the butt of the gun at his waist. 'If we wait much longer, he'll he able to collect some of the old bunch to him and we'll not find it so easy then.'

'Precisely, and I believe this can be done.' Wilder rose to his feet, crossed to the window. 'Better saddle up men. We're ridin' into town. From what I've heard, this *hombre* is somethin' of a dude, spent most of his time carousin' south of the Texas line. Carries no guns and probably figures that this is goin' to save him if he comes up against a gunslick.'

'You reckonin' on gettin' somebody to shoot him down?' mused Dunson. He gave a smoothly vicious grin.

'I'm reckonin' on nothin' of the kind,' snapped Wilder. 'But I do know that he's the kind of man who doesn't like anythin' said against his father. Now if we was to get somebody to speak up against him in the saloon, within Ranson's hearin', and there was to be a fist fight, I reckon we might be able to arrange it so that Ranson came off worst.'

'You talkin' about Brander, your foreman?'

'Why not? He's killed a couple of men in a fist fight that I know of. No reason why there shouldn't be a third.'

Dunson grinned broadly, nodded in agreement. He followed Wilder and the sheriff out into the courtyard, then over to the corral where their horses were waiting. Minutes later, they had ridden out of the ranch yard, leaving behind them the long, slowly-settling streamers of grey dust in the still air.

*   *   *

Chris Ranson felt the tension in the air the minute he thrust open the doors of the saloon and stepped inside, out of the direct heat of the noon sun. The air over the town held the heat-head in it as if unwilling to let it loose, trapping the oven-like quality of it until it brought the sweat boiling out of a man's skin and a dull, throbbing ache to the back of his eyes, an ache brought on by the long staring at the brightly, glaring sunlight.

There were several men already in the saloon, a small group standing at the bar talking together in low tones. He recognised the sheriff with them and two other men he hadn't seen before. One, a tall, frock-coated man with side whiskers and a handsome, if cruel face, threw him a quick, searching look as he walked in, a glance that made to brush over his face, but clung, probing, as if trying to see what lay behind the expression on his face. Chris met the other's hard stare and it was the other's gaze that slid away as Chris walked slowly to the bar, rested his elbows on it, ignoring the group, although still conscious of their presence.

There was a look on the barkeep's face which indicated that he expected trouble and Chris felt the tension rise a little more in him. These men had seen far too many fights in the saloon not to know when one was about to break, but he was still a little unsure of the direction from which the danger would come. It was as if events had begun to crowd him from the moment he had stepped through the door of the saloon and this was something he didn't like, this feeling riding him. He lifted a finger to the barkeep and the man came over with the bottle and a glass, poured the drink for him, took the coin he flipped on to the bar, then stood back, resting his shoulders against the shelf lined with multi-coloured bottles, just below the long mirror.

Silhouetted in the glass, Chris was able to watch every one at his back. The men seated at the tables scattered throughout the room were pointedly ignoring all that went on at the bar, and this was so obvious that he knew, with a sudden certainty, that trouble would come from the group not far from him on his left. Already, there was a sharp burst of hoarse laughter from the frock-coated man as one man said something in low tones.

Chris sipped his drink slowly. The talk from nearby was beginning to get louder.

Suddenly, the tall, broad-shouldered man, with his back to him, said sharply, loudly, 'I don't care what you say, Sheriff. Jim Ranson may have been tough, fast on the draw, but his son was a yeller-livered coward. He ran away to Mexico the minute things got tough and nobody seen hair nor hide of him since then.'

Chris felt the fingers of his hand tighten convulsively around the glass in front of him. There had been a taunting ring to the other's voice which told him, more than the words, that the other had intended he should hear.

The sheriff said something in a low tone, motioned with his thumb in Chris's direction. Chris caught the movement with the edge of his vision, knew that this was also just part of the act, felt the tightness grow in him again, tensing the muscles of his body.

The big man said hoarsely: 'I ain't carin' who's listenin' to me, Maxwell. I'm sayin' exactly what I know to be the truth. Will Ranson ran away because he was scared. He never dared carry a gun in his life for fear that he might have to use it. All he was good for, was as a card-sharp, cheatin' folk at poker and — '

Chris swung around to face the others. His voice was as cutting as the lash of a whip. 'Maybe you're just shootin' off your mouth, mister,' he said thinly. 'But you're a liar. My father was no coward and no cheat.'

The big man turned slowly, eyed him up and down, with a sneering look on his face. He was a tall, solid shape, burned a dark brown by weather and sun; a hard one, scarred by trouble, looking for trouble, evidently still wanting it. During the past ten years, Chris had seen many men like this one, hard and restless, born killers, narrow of mind and governed by passion, hungering for a chance to use their fists and beat a man into a senseless pulp. There was that bright shine in the man's eyes and that twisted look about his thin-lipped mouth that told Chris all that he wanted to know about the other.

'You callin' me a liar, mister?' There was menace in the other's tone as he took a step away from the bar, his hands clear of his body. His gaze swung up and down Chris's body then he looked aside and a glance passed between him and the tall, frock-coated man.

Chris moved slowly forward. The

men at the tables had moved away, stumbling to get out of the way, not sure whether or not bullets would begin to fly at any moment.

'I say that you're a liar if you call my father a coward and a cheat,' Chris repeated tightly.

The other's brows lifted a little as if in mild surprise. 'So you're Ranson. I figured you might be from the way you act. I see you carry no guns. But like your father, that ain't goin' to save you. I can take you apart with my bare hands.' Moving slowly and deliberately, the other unbuckled the heavy gunbelt from around his middle, handed it over to the sheriff. He squared himself at Chris, moving forward in a low crouch, balanced on the balls of his feet.

As he came towards Chris, the other said softly: 'Seems nobody had the chance to take care of your father, but this is where you get what's comin' to you. We don't want the likes of you around here and — ' He never finished what he meant to say. His talk had been merely a feint to cover up his next move. His right hand swung all the way from his belt, aimed for Chris's jaw, but the other was ready for the move. His head scarcely seemed to shift at all, but it was not there when the blow should have landed and the man swayed off balance, falling against Chris, arms outflung as he tried to steady himself. He caught Chris round the middle, hung on to protect himself and brought the top of his head up hard under the other's jaw. Chris felt the shock of the blow roar up into his brain and he was carried back against the bar with the weight of the other, thrusting against his chest, threatening to crush all of the wind from his lungs. With an effort, he shook the ringing sensation from his head, clearing it a little, twisted his body swiftly and instinctively, to one side, knowing what the other intended to do next. He guessed that this man would be a dirty fighter, that he had been brought up in the rough-and-tumble school. The blow which the other aimed with his knee for his crotch, glanced harmlessly off the side of the thigh and the big man uttered a sharp bleat of pain as his knee caught the solid, unyielding wood of the bar.

The pain of the impact forced the other to slacken his grip slightly around Chris's waist and he whirled free of him, swinging a short, hard jab to the gunman's jaw as he moved back. His knuckles rasped along hard flesh, glanced off the cheek bone with a jarring numbness. But the other staggered back under the force of the blow, arms flailing wildly.

Dimly, Chris was aware of the frock-coated man's voice saying: 'Make sure you do a good job on him, Brander. I don't want him walkin' around after this.'

So that was it! A savage anger burned through Chris at the other's words. They had deliberately staged this so that they might get rid of him without having any awkward questions asked. There would be no gunplay. There would be no shooting down of an unarmed man in cold blood. He guessed that the man in the black coat was Matt Wilder. He cursed himself for not having realised that before. The man he faced was undoubtedly a killer with his fists otherwise they would not have been so sure of themselves as to do this in public.

Chris stood away from Brander, facing up to him, waiting for the other to move in. The anger that boiled up inside him was held in tight control as he kept his gaze fixed hard on the man's face, watching his eyes. This was a man who was so sure of himself that he gave a forward indication of what he meant to do, so utterly confident that he would be able to beat any man to a bloody pulp. Snarling fiercely, Brander regained his balance, came stalking forward, arms swinging slightly by his sides, lips drawn back tightly over his teeth, fingers hooked into claws as if he already had Chris's neck in them, was squeezing the life out of him.

Savagely, he swung with his left, throwing all of his weight behind the punch. It grazed Chris's cheek as he swayed back out of reach and before the other could check his onward rush, Chris had sent in two hard jabs to the man's stomach, felt his doubled fists crush into the other's belly, heard the breath gasp out of him in a shrill bleat of agony.

By now, there was a hush on the room. The men standing around the tables could scarcely believe their eyes, that the great Brander, the man who claimed to have already killed two men with his bare hands, was being whipped like this by a man they had considered to be nothing but a dude. Eyes wide, they watched as two more ramrod blows burst against Brander's temple, hitting a little too high up to do any real damage, but stopping him in his tracks, jolting him back on his heels and making him pause in his bull-like rushes.

Chris waited calmly for the other to

come in once more. There was hardly a mark on him, apart from the flush on his neck where the top of the other's head had hammered against it during the first ten seconds of the fight. In contrast, Brander's face bore several marks of the punishing battle. There was an angry flush down one side of his face and a puffiness under his eyes which had not been there a few moments earlier. His lower lip, too, seemed to have become more swollen where Chris's fists had hammered a brief, squashing blow against it, where Brander's teeth had bitten deeply into it, bringing the taste of blood into his mouth.

Brander came forward again, marked but seemingly not badly hurt by the blows. Built solidly, any blows to the chest had little effect on him and Chris had wisely decided to concentrate on the other's belly and face. Crowding him, trying to use all of his tremendous advantage in weight, Brander thrust himself forward, caught out at Chris's arm, swung him round savagely. Wisely, Chris went with the blow — to have tried to withstand it would have meant a broken arm — but as he slid along the polished front of the bar, Sheriff Maxwell thrust out a foot, tripped him so that he fell backward, his shoulders striking the hard, sawdust covered floor of the bar with a stunning force. For a second, all of the air was driven from his chest and he felt as though his lungs had been caved in under the blow. Through a blurring of tears, he saw Brander leap forward with a savage grin of triumph on his face, aiming the kick for the small of Chris's back. Desperately, he tried to roll clear of the blow, but the toe of the other's heavy boot struck him on the side and a savage burst of pain exploded inside his body, lancing up through his chest and into his brain.

For a moment, he lay there, utterly unable to move, aware of the grinning faces of the men standing by the bar, leering down at him, vaguely hearing the sudden roar from them as they urged the other on to the kill. But it was this supreme confidence, the feeling that nothing could stop him now, which proved to be Brander's undoing. He drew back his foot for the death-dealing kick, aiming it for the prostrate man's kidneys, lips showing the uneven teeth.

But the other's pause had given Chris the chance he wanted, those few precious seconds in which to clear his head of the bursting, throbbing ache which had threatened to overwhelm him. This time, instead of trying to wriggle away from the blow, he moved towards it, hands reaching up, fingers grasping around the other's ankle, holding on with all of his strength, pulling sharply to one side.

With a wild yell, Brander teetered on one foot for a moment, then fell sideways, crashing on to the floor beside Chris. Ignoring the pain which lanced through his body, forcing air down into his aching, tortured lungs, Chris forced himself onto his hands and knees, releasing his hold on the other's foot as he struggled to get upright, knowing that he had to get to his feet before the other could collect his scattered wits.

Standing back, resting himself against the bar, knowing that the other men would not dare to shoot him down, not with so many of the townsfolk looking on, he took advantage of the brief respite to breathe slowly and evenly, forcing his thudding, racing heart into a more normal beat inside his ribs. His body felt bruised and battered, and there was that sharp, shooting agony in the lower part of his back. But his vision was clearing and he stared down at the inert figure of the man in front of him, wondering if he would get up again.

Slowly, Brander was clawing himself upright. When he finally swayed erect, arms hanging by his sides, his face was a bloodied mask. It trickled from his nose and the broken lip, smeared over his face, mingled with the sawdust that had formed a mask. His eyes, puffed by the effect of earlier blows, stared at him with a feral hatred and he still came on, prompted only by the savage passion, the desire to kill.

Grinning a little, Chris stood and waited for him, noticing how the other was breathing more slowly now, his great barrel chest heaving with the effort. Too late, he saw that the other held something in his right hand. Even as he moved away from the bar, Brander threw the handful of sawdust into his face. There was no time to move away, no time to think or close his eyes instinctively. The sawdust hit him full in the face, blinding him. With a wild yell, Brander lunged forward, throwing his arms around Chris's waist. Desperately, the other tried to blink the sweat and sawdust from his stinging, tear-filled eyes, unable to rub them as his arms were pinned to his sides.

He could feel the other's foul breath on his face, in his nostrils, as the man tightened his grip around him, locking his fingers around the small of his back, crushing the air and then the life out of his body. This was the kind of fighting the other liked, what he had been trying to do ever since the fight had started, using his superior weight and strength to crush Chris. Desperately, Chris tried to loosen the anaconda-like grip around his body, knowing that his spine would only take so much before it snapped like a rotten twig. The other was beginning to force him back, bending him inexorably. The sheriff yelled something, but the words simply roared through Chris's brain, making no sense. All that he was aware of, was the terrible pressure which was beginning to make his senses reel, the tremendous pain in his back. He knew inwardly that he had somehow to break that hold very soon, or he would be finished and these men would have won. There would be no one to stop them from taking over the ranch and all of that grassland, and the name of Ranson would be finished here, gone from

Cochise County.

The thought gave him a sudden surge of angry strength. He relaxed a little in the other's clinging arms, felt the man shift his stance slightly for that last surge of strength which would finish him. In that same second Chris dropped, bending his knees, felt the other's grip loosen at this sudden and unexpected move, then surged upward, thrusting out with his arms as he did so.

He brought his knee up, felt it hammer against the other's stomach, heard the explosive rush of air from the broken, bleeding lips as Brander staggered back, clutching at his stomach, retching with the pain.

This time, Chris did not pause to give the other a chance to get back his breath, but moved after him, lifted his right arm and brought it down with all of his might across the back of the other's neck. It was a blow that would have killed most men. As it was, there was a bone-jarring crack and Brander dropped without a murmur on to his face at his feet, lay still on the floor, utterly knocked out by the savage force of the blow.

Slowly, sucking air down into his starved lungs, Chris swung to face the men at the bar, his lips drawn back thinly over his teeth. Harshly he said: 'I reckon that takes care of this killer. Any of you figuring on startin' somethin' more?'

For several seconds, there was no move from any of the men there. Then with a harsh grunt, Wilder swung around, pulled a Colt from the holster at his waist and levelled the long barrel on Chris's chest. There was a fanatical glint in his eye as he hissed: 'If we don't finish you one way, I'm damned if I won't make sure with this.' His finger whitened with the pressure he was exerting on the trigger and Chris knew that he was facing a man who would do exactly as he said, who would stop at nothing now that his original plan had failed.

Nothing, he thought numbly, could

stop the other from pulling that trigger and sending him into eternity; nothing at all.

Then, quite abruptly, a voice from the doorway said sharply: 'Put up that gun, Wilder, or by God, I swear I'll kill you. The people of this town will stand for a lot from men such as you, but cold-blooded murder is somethin' different.'

For a second, the thought of trying to turn and beat the other to the shot, lived in Wilder's face. Then he evidently decided better of it, lowered the gun, then thrust it back into the holster, pulled the heavy black coat back over it.

'I'll finish this little episode with you later, Fordham,' he said tightly. He whirled away from the bar, moving towards the door, brushing past the tall figure of Doc Fordham who stood there with the ancient Colt still held firmly in his right hand, his eyes watchful. Reaching the door, Wilder turned in the opening and said harshly: 'Bring Brander along with you, boys. We'll finish this some other time.'

The sheriff and the other man with him bent and picked up the still unconscious man from the floor and staggered out with him. The doors swung shut behind them and Chris leaned back with his elbows propped up on the bar at his back, surveying the scene in front of him. Most of the men went back almost sheepishly to their tables, taking care to avert their gaze from Chris's as he eyed them tightly. The doctor came over and motioned to the barkeep.

'Better drink this up,' he said quietly, handing the glass to Chris. 'You look as though you need it. How did that start?'

'It was all framed, a trap for me to step right into. They'd brought that man with them for the express purpose of killin' me. Like a fool I walked right in with both feet.'

'That's the way these men work. They didn't dare shoot you down without any warnin'. Too many of the people still remember your grandfather and they wouldn't let a thing like that pass. But being killed or badly mauled in a fist fight is somethin' different, even if it was a fight with Brander. He's killed two men like that so far as I know and there may have been more.'

'And I was set up to be number three,' grunted Chris harshly. He drank the whiskey down in a single gulp, almost choked as the raw spirit hit the back of his throat, but it shocked some of the feeling back into his bruised and battered body and a moment later, he was able to think more clearly.

'I guess that now you know a little of what you're up against if you persist in goin' through with your plan and stayin' here,' murmured the other. He poured them both a second drink, then led the way over to one of the tables. 'Get that inside you,' he said quietly, 'and then I'll take you along to my place and strap you up. Wouldn't surprise me none if you ain't got a couple of ribs broken — or at least, cracked, after that brawl. But I guess you're luckier than most. Never figured I'd see the day when Brander was bested in a fist fight.'

'What made you step in like that?' asked Chris tightly. 'This is no quarrel of yours and you said that a man shouldn't take part in another man's quarrel.'

'Let's say that I don't like to stand by and see another man shot down without any chance at all of defending himself.'

Chris drank the second whiskey more slowly than the first. The pain in his body had now subsided into a diffuse ache that had spread to every part of it so that it was impossible to say that it was now located in any particular limb. If anything, this ache was even more difficult to bear than the pain.

When he had finished his drink, the other took him by the arm, gave the bunch of men at the nearby table a quick, almost scathing, glance, and helped him out of the saloon, along the street, to his surgery. Once inside, he locked the door and got to work, washing and bandaging Chris's chest and back.

'You're lucky,' he said finally, when he had finished. 'No bones broken, and only a couple of ribs bruised. I doubt if the same can be said for Brander. You know that you must have nearly killed him.'

'He had it coming,' grunted Chris. He lay back on the low bed, staring up at the ceiling of the room, lips pressed tightly together.

'He'll make a powerful and dangerous enemy,' warned the other, fastening the bag which contained his surgical instruments. 'He'll do anythin' that Wilder asks of him now, just to get even with you. You've beaten him in public and he'll never forget that.'

'At least I know where I stand with him,' nodded Chris. He made to swing his legs to the floor and get up, but the other pushed him back, gently but firmly.

'Where do you think you're goin'?'

asked Fordham.

'Back to the hotel,' protested Chris. 'Where else?'

'You'll be doin' no such thing,' muttered the other in a tone that brooked no argument. 'You'll be stayin' here for the next couple of days until those deep lacerations have healed. Then I might consider lettin' you go back there.'

'But you don't understand. I have to ride out to the ranch tomorrow, otherwise there may be — '

'Surely the ranch has got on all right without you for three weeks since your grandfather died. I reckon it can go without you for another two days.'

Chris sighed, then nodded, giving in. What the other said made sense, of course, but there was still that deep-rooted sense of urgency riding him, an urgency which had been heightened by what had happened in the saloon, the incident bringing home to him the need for speed if he was to take the ranch and hold it, because he felt certain that

Wilder did not intend to stand still now. He would be formulating fresh plans, seeking to put them into operation.

'I'll get somebody to come along and look after you,' promised the other. 'All you have to do is lie here and get some rest. If anythin' happens, I'll let you know right away.'

It was later that evening, when Chris heard the outer door of the office open. Doc Fordham had been out seeing his patients most of the day and Chris guessed that this was the other returning.

'That you, Doc?' he called loudly. He felt a trifle unsure of himself. It hadn't sounded like the other's heavy footfall in the passage outside the door of the room. There was a pause and then the door of the room opened and a girl stepped inside. Chris lay back on the bed, watching her curiously. She walked over and stood beside the bed, looking down at him. There was a faint smile on her face. 'I'm sorry if I startled you,' she said in a low, musical voice, 'but Doctor

Fordham asked me to look in and see how you were. I'm Rosalie Blane.'

'I suppose you already know who I am,' he said quietly, sinking back on to the pillow.

She nodded, unperturbed. 'You're Chris Ranson.' She spread the sheets more evenly over the bed, her manner of crisp assurance returning a little. He knew that she had been a little unsure of herself the moment she had stepped into the room, but no longer. 'They're saying that you fought Brander, the Wilder ranch foreman, and beat him. That must have been something.'

'You seem mighty interested in this,' murmured Chris. The light from the lamp on the nearby table threw shadows over her face, high-lighted the glints in her blue-black hair and the darkness in her eyes. Her lips moved slightly as they curved into a warm smile.

'There's been a lot of talk about you in town and it started long before you rode in. They reckoned that you were just a dude, that even if you did come here you'd simply sell out the ranch and go back south.'

'And would it have made any difference to anyone here if I had?' he inquired.

She nodded, brought him a glass of water, lifted it to his lips. 'It would have meant a lot to the small ranchers in the territory. They looked to your grandfather to protect them against killers like Wilder and Diego. He was the only man here they could really trust, the only man big enough to stand up to them. Without him, they would have been forced off their land many years ago. When he died, they didn't know what to do. There was talk of banding together and forming themselves into some sort of fighting force, knowing that separately they were finished. Then they figured it might be best to wait and see what sort of a man his grandson turned out to be.'

'I see.' He looked at her close and careful, puzzled. She was something of a mystery to him at the moment, not smiling at him now but deadly serious. 'And once they've made up their minds on that score, what do they mean to do?'

'Fight Wilder and Diego. It's the only thing they can do if they want to keep what they have. If they don't, they'll be run out of the territory.'

'And they're lookin' to me to fight their battles for 'em?' He tried to keep the tight bitterness from his voice, but the girl looked up sharply and he saw her lips go tight together.

'All they ask is that you should help them as your grandfather did,' she retorted. 'My father was one of those small ranchers. We had maybe five hundred head of cattle and a couple of hundred acres of land. It wasn't much, but we built a ranch there and it was all that we asked out of life, just to be left alone to live there in peace. But Matthew Wilder wasn't content to let things stay like that. He claimed that we had water on our land that he needed to raise his own cattle. My father said he could have as much of the water as he needed, but that wasn't enough for him. He wanted the land, and the cattle, offered a sum of money that wouldn't even have bought the house and when my father refused point blank to sell, he sent his men early one morning. They fired the barns, and then the house, drove off the cattle and shot my father in the back when he ran out to try to stop them. They would have killed me too but I was trapped in the barn and only managed to get out by the skin of my teeth.'

'Then I can understand why you want to see them finished,' said Chris evenly. 'I can see why you would use every means you could to get revenge on these men.'

'Revenge?' There was a faint note of scorn in her voice and she took a step back from the bed. 'Is that what you think it is? You think I'm just wanting to use you to get revenge on these men.'

'At the moment,' Chris said quietly,

'I don't know what to think. I've been warned so many times that if I don't get my horse and ride out of here, go back to where I came from, my life won't be worth a plugged nickel. You want me to stay but only, it seems, to prevent Wilder and Diego from running the small ranchers off their land.'

The girl remained silent over the long minutes, her face indrawn and sober as she looked into his face. When she finally spoke, her voice held a drag of sadness. 'I thought when I heard what had happened in the saloon, that here was a man who was so like his grandfather that we had nothing more to worry about. I was so glad when I thought that perhaps we now had the chance we've been waiting for to clean up this place, to bring law and order, and justice, back into this part of the territory.' She drew herself up to her full height. Then she turned on her heel and moved towards the door, pausing as she opened it. 'It seems I was wrong,' she said wearily. A moment later, she was gone. He heard her move softly along the passage and then the street door closed quietly behind her. Only the faint, subtle, perfume of her still hung in the room.

Wearily, Chris lay back on the bed and scowled up at the ceiling. He felt angry, not only at himself, but at the fact that there were so many people here who only wanted to use him to gain their own ends, to get something for themselves for which they seemed unwilling to fight and risk their own lives.

He was asleep when the doctor came back, an hour later, and the other did not disturb him, knowing that in his present condition he needed all of the sleep and rest he could get.

It was morning when he woke, the bandages across his ribs making his movement stiff but most of the ache had gone from his body and his mind seemed clear.

3

Gun Thunder

On the second morning, Chris rose early. The night's chill still lay on the room and in spite of himself, his teeth chattered as he dressed as quickly as he could, conscious of the bruising and battering his body had received. There was a pan of warm water which the doctor had brought for him and he shaved with it, the tough whiskers on his face pulling hard against the edge of the razor. There was no other sound of activity in the house and he guessed that Doc Fordham had left on one of his errands. In a town such as this, with only the one doctor, there were bound to be plenty of patients calling him out in an emergency.

Outside, the street was empty and there was the dimness that came before the dawn lying over the town. As he turned the corner and made his way toward the livery stable a man seated on a long, low buckboard, shoulders and head hunched forward against the biting cold, rode by, and there were two others at the far end of the street, loading bags of grain on to other wagons from one of the warehouses. He passed the saloon where Brander had tried to kill him and walked on, shivering as the air bit deep into his bones. He had lain too long in that bed to be able to come out into this without it having this effect on him.

A couple of dogs, their ribs showing like washboards, ran out of the stables as he came up to them. For a moment, he paused to make a smoke and light it up before going in. There was activity inside the stable. Chris saw nothing of the man he had given his mount to when he had arrived, but a gaunt-faced, unkempt man came shuffling out from the stalls at the back, looked him up and down with a brief glance that held nothing of curiosity, then walked over with the horse he was leading and stood by the water trough while it drank.

'Clem ain't here yet,' said the other without turning his head.

'He the groom?'

'That's right.' The other finished watering the horse, turned. 'You must be Jim Ranson's grandson. Heard about what you did to Brander in the saloon the other day. Wish I'd been there and seen it for myself. Always wanted to see that *hombre* get what he deserved, but never figgered I would.' He grinned slyly. 'Reckon you'd better have eyes in the back of your head, mister. He'll shoot you down the first chance he gets and he won't give you any warnin'.'

'So I've been hearin'.' He followed the other as the hostler led the watered horse back to the stall. Putting the horse in one of the stalls, the other slid the long wooden bolt into place, then turned to face Chris.

'You wantin' your own horse?' he asked perkily.

'Not right now,' Chris said. 'I'll be needin' him around noon. How long will it take me to ride out to the ranch?'

'I figger you could make it in an hour,' said the other musingly. His eyes were of the palest, watery blue that Chris had seen and he had the habit of not looking straight at you when he spoke, letting his gaze slide away as if afraid to face you.

'I hear tell that there are a lot of men after that ranch.' Chris rested his arms along the edge of one of the stalls, drawing the smoke from his cigarette down into his lungs. 'Powerful men.'

'That's right. Wouldn't surprise me if they ain't gettin' ready to ride right now.'

Chris said nothing. He had hoped that there might be time in which he could make some plans of his own to meet these men, but it seemed that time was at a high premium as far as he was concerned.

*   *   *

The heat struck him with a savage, built-up intensity as Chris rode out of town and took the trail that led through the low hills which lay to the north. The powdery dust of the trail hung in the air, churned up by the hoofs of his mount and others that had gone before him. He followed the trail as it led up the rising curve of a hill and on its far slope found himself looking down into a wide valley which stretched away almost as far as the eye could see, certainly beyond the wide river to the blue hills that lifted on the far horizon.

The river glinted brilliantly now in the hot sunlight and he could just make out the vast herd of cattle grazing peaceably on the gently rising ground on the far bank. The ranch buildings were visible in the sun-hazed distance, clustered together within sight of the river.

He halted his mount on the rocky outcrop of ground that jutted out from the side of the hill, sat tall and straight in the saddle, feeling the heat on his back and shoulders, listening to the afternoon's great silence, conscious more than ever of the vast blue reaches of the sky over his head; a deep blue vault in which only the glaring disc of the noon sun burned and, looking down at the land which he only vaguely remembered from a dim and distant past, he felt the deep stirrings of emotion within him. Close to him, on the slope, shaded by the outstretching arms of the big cottonwood trees, a narrow creek tumbled noisily over the flat, smooth stones that glistened and shone whitely on the bed of sand. Nothing seemed to ever disturb the utter peace here and he felt that one had only to stand there long enough to be able to hear the Voice of God speaking out over the vastnesses of the great country.

Gripping himself, he pulled his mind away from the majesty of the scene, forced himself to concentrate on the nagging worries that tugged at the back of his thoughts and kept the tautness in him. Maybe, after all, his mission here would prove to be pointless. He had learned much since he had ridden into this territory. It was a land divided with Matt Wilder on one side of the fence, Diego on the other — and nothing in between for the lesser men now that his grandfather was dead. He knew they were looking desperately to him to fill the vacuum left by the old man's death, to step in and take over where he had left off. But killing other men was a big thing as far as he was concerned; a problem that a man could deal with only as he saw fit.

He raked the rowels over the flanks of his mount, pulling its head around sharply, let it take its own time and find its own way down the twisting, rocky trail. There was smoke rising from the chimney of the ranch house as he rode into the courtyard, slid from the saddle and let his mount run into the corral, closing the gate after it. Who would be there at this time of the afternoon? he wondered; unless it was someone who knew of his coming and had wanted to put the place into some kind of shape for his homecoming.

Making his way over the dusty courtyard, he paused for a moment outside the door, feeling all of the memories which he had thought were long since forgotten, come flooding over him again in a tremendous wave. This was the place he had known intimately for the first nine years of his life. Had it not been for the bitter quarrel between his father and grandfather, he might have stayed there for the rest of his life, instead of running off to Mexico.

Opening the door and stepping inside, he found himself in the well-remembered hallway with the old pictures on the wall. Nothing seemed to have changed in the slightest. It was as if he had left home and then returned the next day, instead of there having been almost thirteen years in between. There was a movement in the room which led off the corridor and he swung round sharply as the door opened, then stared in amazement. The girl stepped out into the passage, gazing frankly at him.

The moment's tension reacted strongly and sharply in Chris. He spoke half-angrily. 'I thought that I'd given you to understand — '

'I know what you're going to say, and I'm sorry for what I said the other day,' put in the girl quickly. 'I came here to see if there was anything I could do to help. Since your grandfather died, this place has had nothing done to it and — '

Once again, Chris stared in surprise. The silence lengthened and he found himself thinking how cool it was in here, in contrast to the tremendous heat in the air outside. Forcing a faint smile, he moved forward and followed her into the large parlour. The knowledge of how he had spoken so roughly to her on their last meeting rested heavily on him.

Crossing to the window, he stood for a long moment with his back to her, peering out into the courtyard, out to the corral where more than a score of work-broke horses moved between the circular fences.

'I think I know how you feel about this place,' said the girl from behind him. She came over and stood beside him, looking out towards the distant hills which marked the southern boundary of the spread. 'Your grandfather and my father were friends, perhaps each was the only real friend that the other had. When they both died, I came here to try to look after the place. I'd come to look on it as my home. Believe me, I've had a hard time keeping hired hands here. They seem to have heard a lot of stories about you — and they never bothered to check on whether there was any truth in them or not. Whenever any of Wilder's men started spreading rumours, they were readily believed.'

'And what do you think?' he asked, his voice strangely cold and distant. He saw her looking at him and he had the idea that she wanted desperately to trust him but was not sure whether she could.

'Running away from responsibilities is a pretty small thing for a man to do,' she said finally, weighing her words with care. 'You'll find that if you ride out and leave the small ranchers to the tender mercies of Wilder and Diego, you can never run far enough to get away from your own conscience.' She shrugged her shoulders. 'Never mind, though. It's your business, I suppose; and nothing really to do with me. But you can see how things are going, can't you?'

'The ranchers would be strong enough to stand up to these killers, if they only had the sense and the courage to bunch together and force the issue.'

'These people did not come here with the idea of having to fight for what they bought legally, and which they've built over the years with their bare hands. All that they've ever asked is to be left in peace. But Wilder hates all of the small people, believes that this country can never thrive properly unless it's ruled by one man, a strong and ruthless man.'

'Namely, Matthew Wilder.'

'Exactly. He's a greedy man who wants wealth and power more than anything else in this world and he doesn't care how he gets it.'

'All men are greedy in one way or another,' said Chris musingly.

She gave him a sharp, keen glance, suddenly arrested by that remark, then turned away from the window, walking back into the room and standing in front of the small table. 'I wonder just how deep that hatred of violence really goes in you?' she murmured. 'How much it is going to take before you see things as they really are, before you discover that to be any sort of man at all in this country, you have to fight and risk your neck. You don't have the face of a man who seeks only pleasure out of this life. Are you sure that you're as dead set against violence as you would have everyone believe?'

'Does that really matter so much to you?'

'Yes, I think it does,' she said, her voice a little too casual. 'I knew your grandfather very well. He might have been my grandfather instead of yours; and all his life, he tried to do what he could for men less fortunate than himself. Oh, I know he tried never to show it. He, too, believed that doing good was a show of weakness that was unbecoming of a man. But nevertheless, he stood behind these men, facing up to Wilder and the others whenever they tried to move in. I hoped that for his memory, you would turn out to be the same kind of man, that you wouldn't simply stand by, doing nothing, while these men have their homes and spreads burned down about their ears, their wives and families shot by gunmen, because they refused to sell their ranches at a ridiculously low price.'

She bit her lower lip in indecision, for a moment, then went on: 'I can remember the time, not long ago, when I could ride out across the range and up into the hills without carrying a gun, without any fear at all. But that isn't so now. I always have to expect the worst from every bend in the trail.' She paused and looked up curiously. 'You would ride along the hill trail out of town when you came here?'

He nodded. 'That's right. But I never saw anybody there who represented any danger to me.'

'But don't you agree that this is one of the most beautiful, clean stretches of country that you've ever seen?'

He said: 'I don't think there's any point in denying that.'

'Yet you'd stand by, willingly, and see this terrible evil come to so beautiful a stretch of land.'

Once again, Chris felt himself caught by surprise. Quietly, he said: 'I'll attend to any chores I have, but I fail to see why I should carry out those of any other man.' He felt a wave of bitter anger in him, directed more against himself than against the girl. After all, he thought inwardly, she had lived here all of these years and knew what was happening.

He went back to the table where she stood, then glanced down at what lay on the smoothly polished surface. For an instant, there was a touch of ice trailing down his spine.

The girl said softly: 'Those are your grandfather's guns, Chris. He always wore them when he rode around the ranch, or into town. They've killed men but all in fair fight. I thought you might like to have them, seeing as you have the right to them.' She twisted her lips into a faint, half-hearted smile, as if unsure of herself and what she had done.

Chris stared down at the guns in

their leather holsters, at the smooth metal that shone in the bright sunlight which streamed through the open window. They spoke to him with their own voices and told of things that he did not like.

'I don't see why you should — ' he began, then stopped abruptly at a sudden sound outside. Thinking back, he realised that he must have been vaguely aware of the sound of riders coming closer to the ranch, cutting in over the stretching grassland, but he had paid little attention to it, supposing that there were still plenty of men around, waiting to see how events would turn out, men who had served under his grandfather. Even as he started for the window, he heard a man outside yell, loud and long, in warning and a second later, there came a sudden flurry of gunshots, sharp and angry in the quietness outside the ranch house.

'What is it?' asked the girl quickly. She came forward, then pressed herself against the wall of the room as a shot came splintering through the window and bedded itself in the wall of the other side. The move outside had taken Chris completely by surprise. The firing swung round, seemed to be concentrated near the big barn some fifty yards from the house itself. It was a savage destruction that seemed to have flared up within moments. Risking a quick look through the smashed glass of the window, he caught sight of the group of men on horseback, milling around at the far end of the courtyard. They were emptying their guns into the barn where some of his own men were trapped. Even as he watched, he saw the three men break away from the main, milling bunch, the lighted torches in their hands, racing their mounts past the narrow opening in the barn, hurling the torches through on to the straw that lay piled high inside.

'They're going to burn those men out,' gasped the girl. She had pushed herself forward, oblivious of the danger she faced, was staring open-mouthed and white-faced, in the direction of the long barn, her eyes wide in horror.

Whirling, Chris ran out of the room, along the passage and threw open the front door. Behind him, he heard the girl shout a quick warning.

Ignoring it, he stepped out into the courtyard, walked purposefully in the direction of the tightly-bunched riders. He was within twenty feet of them before his presence there was noticed. Then one of them gigged his mount forward, pulling out from the others and Chris recognised him immediately; the same black frock-coat, the same handsome but sneering expression.

'I figured you might need a little persuasion, Mister Ranson,' said Wilder sarcastically. 'Here, we don't bargain with dudes or men who don't wear guns. I made your grandfather an offer for this place. Ten thousand dollars. He wouldn't accept it, even went so far as to threaten me.' The sneering lips parted a little more. 'Seems to me that the ranch is in a worse condition now than it was then. You just seem to have lost one of your barns, so my offer is now eight thousand dollars and you can take it or leave it. Only don't expect the offer to stay open for too long. I'm an impatient man and I like to get things done quickly.'

'I gave my answer to that crooked sheriff of yours,' Chris said through tightly-clenched teeth. He fought to keep the savage anger from breaking the bounds of his tight control. 'I don't make bargains with cold-blooded murderers.'

For a moment, he thought the other meant to shoot him down there and then. The long-barrelled Colt in Wilder's right hand levelled on his chest and he saw the finger tighten on the trigger, saw the look of deep anger suffused in the other's face. Then Wilder jerked back his head and laughed harshly. 'Then in that case,' he said thickly, 'we've got nothin' more to discuss. It would be a pity if I had to burn down all of this and shoot every man who works for you, but that's what I'll do if you haven't seen sense in the next couple of days. Forty-eight hours, Ranson and then I'll be back for my answer.'

He pulled hard on the reins, wheeling his mount away. Turning, he paused and looked down. 'Somehow, I don't think you'll get anybody to back you up if you try to stop me. My advice to you is not to waste your time. Ride on out of here while you still have a whole skin.'

Raking rowels across his mount's flanks, he raced the sorrel away over the dusty courtyard, calling to his men to follow him. Even as they rode along the winding trail that led up the side of the hill in the distance, Chris ran for the burning barn. One glance was enough to tell him that there was no chance of saving the building; the fire had gained too firm a hold and the straw there was as dry as tinder. There was scarcely any smoke, only the quivering of the superheated air in the harsh, strong sunlight as the invisible flames licked upward, soaring irresistably towards the roof. Here and there, flames were beginning to sprout from the roof and it was only a matter of minutes before it fell in.

A wall of flame met Chris as he moved towards the blazing doorway. He knew that there were still men trapped inside, caught by the barrier of flame, possibly wounded men who had taken refuge there when those killers had started slinging lead. Swiftly, he tore off his jacket, thrust it into the trough beside the barn until the water dripped from it into a small puddle around his feet, then held it in front of him as a shield, before running through the wall of flame. Heat singed his hair and face, burning his arms. But in a few seconds, he was through, trying to see through the heat haze that brought tears into his eyes, blurring his vision as he strove to make out the figure of any of the men. One lay on the blazing straw less than four feet away, but even as he turned the other over, felt the limp looseness of the man's body, he knew that there would be no need to try to get this man out. The bullet had caught him high in the chest, on the left side, had probably nicked the heart, killing him almost instantly.

Coughing, struggling to breathe, he rushed on into the barn. A blazing beam fell from the roof and crashed on to the floor only a couple of feet in front of him and glancing upward, he saw the huge gap in the roof, the sagging, twisted beams which would fall within a few more moments. Desperately, he tried to hang on to his buckling consciousness. His chest felt as if it were on fire and every breath that he took, sucking it down into his aching, tortured lungs, seemed to be adding fuel to the fire that roared inside him. His lungs seemed to be unable to extract sufficient oxygen from the air to supply his body with its needs and his heart was pumping and racing inside him so that it threatened to burst asunder at every single beat. He knew that he could not stay here much longer, that if he did not get out soon, he would be overcome by the heat and flames and have little chance of getting out alive, even if the roof did not collapse and crush him entirely.

He was on the point of turning back in the direction of the door, when he caught a fragmentary glimpse of the figure over by the far wall, crouched against it, one arm thrown over its face, as if trying to shield the eyes from the searing heat. Reaching the man, he caught at him by the shoulder, saw the other lower his arm as if in surprise, then try to get to his feet, but his leg gave under him as though unable to bear his weight. Glancing down, Chris saw the stain of blood on the other's pants, gritted his teeth, thrust one arm under the injured man's shoulder and half-dragged, half-carried him through the flames. It was impossible to see the door. Tears blinded him and he was forced to narrow his lids until he could see very little. Somehow, he managed to get the other to the door, felt the strength leave him. There were only three more feet to go. Dimly, he could see daylight through the quivering flames, could just make out the confused shouting outside. Then his senses left him. He fell forward, unable to hold up the other any longer. He was not aware of the beams which crashed down behind him, adding their heat to that already inside the barn. He was not aware of the two men who ran in through the open doorway, grasping him and the injured man, lifting them and staggering with them outside.

His first impression was of coolness on his face, of water trickling down his cheeks, dripping from his chin and on to his neck. There was a faint crackling in his ears which he could not recognise and the dull murmur of voices nearby. When he tried to open his eyes, the glaring brightness forced him to close them again. For several moments he lay still, then felt the coldness of glass against his lips as they were gently forced open and something raw and hot was poured down his throat. Coughing and spluttering, he shook his head in an attempt to clear it and this time when he opened his eyes, he forced them to stay open, squinting up at the sun. He turned his head to one side, found himself looking at the girl and the two men with her. The man he had brought out of the blazing barn lay a few feet away.

'Better lie still for a little while,' said Rosalie softly, 'until you've recovered. Then we'll get you into the house.'

He shook his head, pushed himself up on to his hands. There was still a dull throbbing in his forehead, but now that he was able to breathe down great lungfuls of clear, clean air, he felt better. Groggily, he got to his feet, swaying a little as the blood rushed, pounding, to his aching forehead, but waved away the two men as they took a step forward to help him.

'I'm all right now,' he said harshly.

He turned a little and threw a black look in the direction of the barn, now almost completely gutted and destroyed. A few beams smouldered in the centre of the ruin and here and there a tall column of red-edged flame leapt upward as it fed momentarily on a pile of unburnt straw or wood.

He knew that the others were watching him closely, wondering what he intended to do, he felt their eyes on the back of his neck as he turned and walked slowly towards the house. Rosalie made a quick move to follow him, but one of the men put out a restraining hand and shook his head and she fell back again, watching him wonderingly.

The silence that lived in the parlour pounded in Chris's chest as he went in through the open door. The tiny shards of glass from the broken window glittered brilliantly on the carpet under his feet; but he gave them only a cursory glance as he walked, stony-faced, to the table in the middle of the room. He stared at the strange gunbelt on the table, with the twin Colts resting snugly in the leather holsters, the material polished hard and smooth and shiny from the constant rub of metal against it. Any feeling of guilt, of reluctance, which had once been in his mind seemed to have been burned away by the flames inside the blazing barn, seared by the anger that had flooded through him in a savage wave. Reaching out, he ran his fingertips over the hard, cold metal; then his fingers curled about the smooth leather. Slowly and methodically, he put it around his waist and fastened the heavy buckle into place.

★   ★   ★

Night reached in from the east and the reds and scarlets in the west were swiftly swamped by the encroaching darkness that spread itself over the sky. As Chris rode down the twisting mountain trail into town, there was the faint sound of other riders moving in the hills, the dull murmur of hoofbeats reaching out of the clinging, all-enveloping stillness which seemed to come to the country at this hour of the day. Once clear of the crags and boulders, he rode on without hurrying, still trying to put his thoughts into some kind of order. The trail widened where it met the main stage route into town, but he passed no one on the way and there were few people abroad on the boardwalks as he rode along the main street, not pausing until he reached Doc Fordham's office.

Dropping from the saddle, he hitched the reins over the post, climbed up on to the sidewalk and knocked softly on the door. It opened a few moments later and Doc Fordham peered out into the darkness, recognised him, and opened the door wider for him to step inside.

'Glad you came, Chris,' he said genially, opening the door into the parlour. 'I was worried about you when you moved out in spite of my objections. How are the cuts and bruises?'

'Well enough, Doc. But it wasn't about that, that I came to see you.'

The other moved around to the far side of the table, peered closely at Chris in the lamp light. Then his eyes widened just a shade and he nodded to himself as if in secret understanding. 'I think I'm beginning to get the picture,' he said, and he nodded his head slightly towards the guns slung low at Chris's waist. 'Are those your grandfather's guns?'

Chris nodded in silence.

'I thought I recognised 'em. Somethin' has happened, hasn't it?'

'Wilder and some of his hired killers rode into the ranch this afternoon, shortly after I arrived there. They killed two of the men and wounded another, after they'd trapped 'em in the big barn. Then they fired the barn, just as a warnin' to me of what would happen if I didn't give in to them, and sell out at a ridiculous sum.'

'So you've finally come to your senses,' nodded the other. There was a hard glint in his deep-set eyes. 'Do you intend to use those guns? Or are they there just for ornament?'

'If they force me to use 'em, then I will,' said Chris harshly. 'That's why I came to see you. I need your help.'

The other shrugged. 'If you want me to strap on a pair of guns and stand at your shoulders, then I'll do it, but I reckon I ought to warn you that I'm a pretty poor shot and — '

'That isn't the sort of help I want from you,' Chris told him. 'But it seems to me there's only one way to fight Wilder and his crew of hired gunslingers, and that's by usin' force, the same way as they do.'

'Then where do I come in?' asked the other, glancing up at him, the light from the lamp throwing his face into deep shadow.

'Who elected Maxwell as sheriff of the town?'

'Why, we did, I reckon. I mean, the townsfolk. To be quite honest, I think he was the only man for the job. Nobody else would have it. This place had the name of a pretty lawless town in those days and I guess everybody was thinking of their own skin. The only reason Maxwell has lasted so long is that both Wilder and Diego use him.'

'But you could get rid of him if you wanted to, couldn't you, elect another man in his place?'

The other pursed his lips tightly, considering that. 'Wilder isn't goin' to like it if we did that.'

'Damn Wilder!' snapped Chris tightly. 'If there's to be law and order around here, then we've got to make a start somewhere. And the sooner we get rid of that crooked sheriff, the better.'

'You got any suggestions as to who we ought to elect in his place?' The other lifted thick, bushy brows, drawing them into a tight, interrogative line.

'I'll take that job,' said Chris flatly. 'And if it brings things to a showdown quickly, so much the better.'

'And Maxwell — he won't like it either. What do you mean to do with him?'

Chris smiled mirthlessly. 'I reckon that the best place for a crooked lawman such as Maxwell will be in his own jail. There should be plenty of charges we can bring against him, enough to keep him locked away for several years, if not to put a noose around his neck.'

'Now you're talking like that grandfather of yours,' said the other with a trace of enthusiasm in his voice. He reached for his hat hanging near the door. 'Let's get around and have a little talk with Haycock, the banker, and one or two of the others. I figure this oughtn't take long.'

In the Grand Union saloon, it was the dead hour of the evening, the hour when most of its customers were in the hotels, eating their supper, thankful of the evening which had brought coolness to the air, replacing the oven-rawness of the day. Inside the saloon, the bar-room was almost empty. A swamper ran the broom over the floor, clearing away the refuse of the afternoon, ready for the usual influx of men which would begin in less than half an hour's time. He finished his brushing, laid the broom in one corner and pulled the rag from his pocket, wiping down the stains from the bar with a mechanical, half-hearted movement, his actions dull and lethargic, mind blurred from lack of fresh air, the atmosphere inside the bar-room filled with the stale odour of cigars and spilled whiskey. Tossing a couple of empty bottles into the box under the counter, he reached the end of the bar, glanced up at the long mirror on the wall at the back of the room, then swung his glance around quickly as the doors were pushed open and the two men came in.

In the dim light, he recognised Sheriff Maxwell and Brander, Wilder's ranch foreman. For a moment, he busied himself with stacking up the empty glasses that had lined the bar, then glanced up as the two men moved across to him, stood with their elbows hooked on to the bar.

'You're in early tonight, Sheriff,' he said quickly.

Maxwell gave out with a surly scowl, took the bottle from the other with a sharp movement and poured out drinks for Brander and himself. 'You heard that there was a burnin' at the Ranson place?' he asked casually.

The barkeep shook his head. 'I ain't heard nothin' about that,' he said thinly. 'Nobody's been here yet to tell me anythin'. Much damage done?'

The barkeep was a man who had no leanings either way in this duel that was shaping up on the range outside of town. He meant to ensure that he remained neutral, knowing that there would be plenty of money coming into the saloon, whichever side won in the end, and no actions of his would influence either side until the outcome was clear. He did not doubt, for one moment, that with all of the men he had at his back, and the fact that if the stories which he had heard about this grandson of the old man's were true, then Wilder would have little difficulty in running the other off the range and out of the territory. That was, if he did try to stand up and face Wilder. The most sensible thing for him to do, if he valued his skin at all, would be to get his horse and ride back to where he had come from. But even though the outcome did seem to be a virtual certainty, there was still that nagging little suspicion at the back of his mind that perhaps this stranger had more to him than met the eye, and that being the case, he would stay sitting on the fence until he knew for sure which way to jump.

'The boys fired the big barn and shot up a few of the ranch hands there,' declared Brander thickly. He gulped down his drink and poured himself another, tossing it down his throat in a single, swift motion, screwing up his lips as the bite of the raw liquor hit the back of his throat. 'I reckon that should make him realise he's not wanted here.'

'And if he don't feel like runnin'?'

'Then by God, we'll stop him permanently,' put in Maxwell. He lifted the glass of whiskey to his lips, then paused with it halfway there, as if frozen into stone, his wide-open eyes fixed on the mirror at the back of the bar, on the reflection of the men who had stepped into the saloon, the swing doors closing softly at their backs.

'For your trouble, Maxwell,' cut in Chris's voice thinly, 'you can have the chance to finish me permanently right here and now.'

Maxwell whirled, his back to the bar. Brander turned more slowly. If he felt any surprise at hearing Chris's voice behind him, he gave no outward sign. Only the dark eyes narrowed into mere slits and there was hardness to his features, a look of malevolent hatred in his gaze. His face still bore the marks of the beating he had taken from Chris some days before and he put up one hand to his cheek, feeling it instinctively, gingerly, as he faced the other. Then his gaze dropped to the guns at the other's waist and his lips pulled back in a faint sneer.

'You come dressed with guns this time, dude,' he called thickly. 'You sure don't think much of life.'

'I've come to arrest Maxwell,' said Chris flatly. 'On a charge of working in cahoots with Matthew Wilder. There may be more charges when we get around to 'em, but I reckon that should be enough to keep him locked in jail until certain other matters have been taken care of.'

'You ain't got no right to arrest me,' snarled Maxwell. He took a step forward and moved his hand towards the badge on his shirt. 'I'm the law here and I — '

'Not any longer,' broke in Chris tightly. He eased back his jacket a little, to show the star on his own shirt. 'You see, the townsfolk here figured that they want somebody as sheriff who takes his orders from nobody, certainly nobody like Wilder. So they decided you were no longer sheriff here and they elected me in your place — as of now.' His words bit across the clinging silence in the bar-room like the lash of a whip.

'You can't do that,' shouted Maxwell in harsh protest. 'I'm sheriff here and no two-bit tinhorn is goin' to ride in and take over. I'll see you all in Hell first.'

'If you make any move towards your guns, that's where you'll be goin',' cut in Chris.

At that, Brander began a slow drift to one side, keeping his shoulders pressed against the bar, his eyes never once leaving Chris's face. He kept his hands in full view all of the time, but Chris knew that this was a deliberate move on the other's part, that it was as if a pre-arranged signal had passed between these two men, and they were making their move to box him in from two sides when it came to the showdown.

Deliberately, he eyed them with an unfocused gaze, his eyes taking in both of them so that any sudden movement by either of them would be seen at once.

'That's far enough, Brander,' he snapped harshly. 'Now, Maxwell, do you intend to come quietly, or do you want this thing done the hard way?'

'You wouldn't dare draw on me,' said the sheriff. 'You know damned well that you don't stand a chance of getting the drop on us and even if you tried, there are two of us, three if we count the barkeep. I reckon he knows where he'd better stand in this and he always keeps a shotgun just below the counter.' From the way the other spoke, stressing his words, Chris guessed that this was as good as an order to the barkeep, that if he knew what was good for him, he would do exactly as he was told and make a dive for the shotgun — and use it — whenever he, Chris, made his play.

Chris flickered a glance towards the stocky, stolid-faced man behind the bar.

The other still stood there, unmoving, his hands in sight on top of the bar in front of him. Chris prided himself on his knowledge of what other men were likely to do in circumstances such as this and he felt pretty certain that the barkeep would make no move until he saw how things were going. He could discount the other and keep his attention glued to the two men facing him at the bar.

'Somehow, I don't think that man behind you is goin' to take any sides in this little argument,' Chris said finally, as the silence in the bar-room grew long. 'Now I'm tellin' you once again. Toss down your guns and move out of here in front of me. The same goes for you, too, Brander. I've got a charge of murder hangin' over you.'

'You ain't got nothin' on me,' snarled the other. Each finger of his hands was thrust wide, pushing outward like the spoke of a wheel, the hands held inches above the butts of his guns. His eyes were now locked with those of the man who faced them. Waiting, watching, probing for the sign that would indicate that death was on its way. Silence crowded down on the room.

Then, as if at a signal, both Maxwell and Brander went for their guns. Hands swept down, plucking the Colts from leather. But their draw was no match for the man who faced them. Down and up, Chris lifted the long barrels in a sweeping draw that brought the muzzles inches above their line of fire. A single, swift snap of his wrists and sound bucketed through the bar-room. Brander stood upright for a moment, as if stretching up on his toes, head thrust forward, a look of stunned wonder and surprise on his features, his eyes striving to hold life in them. Then he toppled forward, the guns slipping from nerveless fingers, dropping with a clatter to the floor seconds before his huge body crashed down on top of them, to lie unmoving in the newly-swept sawdust.

Beside him, Maxwell lay back, half over the bar, his arms by his sides.

Neither gun had cleared leather when the bullet had hit him high in the shoulder. His face was contorted into a spasm of shocked, stunned agony and the red stain on his shirt was beginning to widen slowly as the cloth soaked up the blood which welled slowly and continuously from the wound.

Chris moved forward, paused in front of the other, thrusting one of the Colts back into its holster, the other lined up on the wounded man's chest.

Without being told again, the other released his hold on the guns and they fell into the sawdust at his feet. Sweat showed on his forehead and trickled down the folds of skin on his flabby cheeks. His eyes were wide, staring, with fear showing deep in them. Reaching forward, Chris grasped the star on the other's shirt as he cringed back, then ripped it off with such force that it tore the material, leaving a gaping rent in the shirt.

'All right,' he said thinly, 'let's go. Over to the jail.'

'You won't get away with this,' muttered the other, as he stumbled forward, out through the swinging doors and along the dark street. 'When Wilder hears about this, he'll send his boys into town to get me out and they'll shoot you down like a dog, whether you're wearin' that badge or not. You don't think the townsfolk here have got any say in what happens, do you?'

'Maybe they hadn't in the past, but we've decided to change a few things as from tonight,' muttered Chris as he prodded the other forward. 'And this is one of those things. Now I reckon you'd better get inside that jail and keep quiet, or this gun may go off. If there's one thing I hate it's a crooked sheriff, a man who hides behind a badge and sells out the people he's hired to protect.'

He thrust the other into one of the small cells at the rear of the jail building, stepped out into the corridor and locked the door behind him.

With an effort, Maxwell got to his

feet and came forward, fingers hooked around the metal bars of the door. 'You're not goin' to leave me in here like this, are you?' he muttered hoarsely. 'What about this slug in my shoulder? You want me to bleed to death in here before mornin'?'

'Wouldn't worry me particularly if you did,' grunted Chris harshly. 'I'll get the doctor to take a look at you as soon as I can get him here.'

★　★　★

When Matthew Wilder came in from the corral, the sun had just lifted itself clear of the eastern skyline and shadows were long in the courtyard as he made his way over to the ranch house, spurs raking up the dust on the ground. The horse that stood near the water trough had been ridden long and hard during the night, its coat streaked with dust, the lather of sweat still on its neck and legs. He gave it a quick glance, then went inside. He went quickly along the narrow passage to the door at the end, thrust it open and stepped inside. Four men were seated in the room. Garvey, Wendell and the two Matson brothers. Wendell got to his feet as Wilder strode into the room, his gaze flicking to each man in turn.

'Somethin' happened?' he asked tersely. He rolled himself a smoke and seated himself in the chair that Wendell had just vacated.

'That's right,' nodded Wendell. 'Somethin' we've got to take care of right away.'

Wilder eyed him in momentary surprise. 'Well,' he asked dryly. 'What's on your minds? Not worried about what Ranson might do after that lesson we taught him yesterday, are you?' He lit the cigarette, blew smoke into the air. 'If you are, then forget it. He'll be running out of the territory any day now with his tail between his legs like a whipped cur.'

Garvey shook his head. 'Ranson ain't goin' to run, Boss,' he said with conviction. 'He's already started to make trouble for us — big trouble.'

Wilder sat up straight in his chair at that, the cigarette forgotten between his fingers, the smoke curling up and lacing painfully across his eyes, but he did not seem to notice. 'What sort of trouble?' he demanded, his voice hard.

'Brander's dead,' put in Wendell. 'Seems this *hombre*, Ranson, put on his grandfather's guns and rode into town shortly after we burned down the barn. He went straight to the townsfolk and got them to elect him sheriff and cut Maxwell out altogether. Then he went to the saloon, threatened to run Maxwell into his own cell on a charge of being in cahoots with you and sellin' out the town. He called 'em both and the barkeep swears that they drew first, but that this *hombre* is like greased lightning with a gun. He shot Brander before he could squeeze off a single shot and plugged Maxwell in the shoulder before his guns had even cleared leather. Maxwell's in jail right now and like I said, Brander's dead.'

A sudden heat showed briefly in Wilder's hard stare. He made to push himself out of the chair, arms braced beside him, then lowered himself down again, forcing himself to relax. 'You're right. We've got to finish him — and fast. Before he can rally any of the others to him. There are several men who remember his grandfather and they might figure on joinin' up with him now that he's shown that he's not such a dude as we reckoned. We made a mistake and it's up to us to rectify it as quickly as we can. Where is he now?' His look challenged Wendell.

'Back in town,' nodded the other. 'I figure he'll stay there until the circuit judge gets here to try Maxwell.'

'That's all the better for us. We've got to get Maxwell out of there before he cracks and does a heap of talkin'. He knows too much of our plans. If he spills it all to Ranson, we may not find it easy to get rid of him.'

'How do you figure we ought to do

it?' asked Garvey.

In answer, Wilder jerked a thumb towards the Matson brothers. 'That's your chore, boys,' he said softly. 'You know what to do.'

They nodded. 'Sure thing, boss. If he's as fast as they say he is, maybe a shot from a dark alley would — '

'Do it any way you like,' retorted the other heatedly. 'All I want now is that Ranson is dead before the mornin' tomorrow.'

Wendell shook his head swiftly. 'It ain't that easy,' he put in. 'Even though he's only been here a few days, already a lot of folk are beginning to swing round to him. We spread that story about his father and that satisfied most of the folk here and they seemed prepared to accept that Chris Ranson was made in the same mould. When he first came here, that impression stuck, but since this happened yesterday, I figure they'll be thinkin' differently. He's a tougher proposition than we figured. A shot in the back — yes, I'd go along with that, but not in any way that could connect it with us.'

'Why not, once he's dead, we've got nothin' to worry about,' snapped Wilder harshly. 'He's mortal like the rest of us and a bullet can kill him as quickly as any other man. If we wait, we may lose more men and with Diego ready to move in once we show any sign of weakness, that's somethin' we can't afford.'

'But if we arranged it so that it appeared one of Diego's men had done it,' muttered Wendell, 'that ought to solve both of our problems.'

'You make sense,' Wilder acknowledged eventually. 'You got any idea how that can be done?'

'Me and Garvey have it figured,' he claimed with conviction in his voice. 'Just leave it to us and you can be sure this *hombre* Ranson won't be any more trouble after tonight.'

'All right. Have it your way. But if there's any slip-up, then — '

'There won't be,' promised the other

152

tightly. He eased himself to his feet from where he had been seated on the arm of Garvey's chair. Motioning to the other, they went out and a few moments later, Wilder heard them ride out of the courtyard and take the trail that led into town. In spite of their assurance that everything would be taken care of, he still felt uneasy in his mind. This news of Brander's death and Maxwell's imprisonment had come as a tremendous shock to him. It was the last thing he had ever expected Ranson to do. That burning down of the barn on his spread and the killing of those men of his must have forced his hand. Certainly that was the only explanation he could offer to himself at the moment.

But if all this were true, and at the moment he saw no reason to doubt it, it meant that he was facing an opponent at least as hard and as fast on the draw as old man Ranson had been. When the other had died, he had expected to be able to move in and take over that ranch without any trouble. If he had been able to do that, he would have become so much bigger and more powerful than Diego, that he might be strong enough to force the other out of the territory. Then he would be the undisputed ruler of this part of the country, his empire would stretch much further than the eye could see in any direction and even the town would be his.

Now he had been forced to rearrange all of his carefully laid plans. If Wendell and Garvey succeeded in what they had set out to do, all so well and good — and his worries would be over. But if not, if they failed as Brander and Maxwell had so clearly failed, then the time would have come for a showdown.

For an instant, he even considered the possibility of teaming up with Diego, until they had rid the place of Ranson, recognising him as a common enemy; but he doubted if Diego would trust him sufficiently to agree to this. He wasn't sure that he could trust Diego.

His glance fell on the Matson brothers and he nodded towards the door. 'Better get back to work,' he said tonelessly, 'and if I need you, I'll call on you.'

When they had gone, he sat stiff and straight in his chair, staring straight out ahead of him, turning his thoughts over in his mind. Why in God's name did this Chris Ranson have to come back and claim this ranch? After all, he hadn't been to this place, hadn't been within several hundred miles of it, for close on thirteen or fourteen years. Now, somehow, the lawyers had succeeded in tracing him and giving him the news of his grandfather's death and he had decided to take the place and begin where his grandfather had left off. It was beginning to look as though the raid on the Ranson spread the previous day had been a big mistake. It might have been better if he had held his hand for the time being, and gone out there to parley with Ranson. At least, it would have been possible to gain time in which to formulate some other plan which might have had a higher chance of success. There was, of course, one possibility that he hadn't considered, but which was obviously worthy of consideration. That girl, Rosalie. She had been hanging around the Ranson place for some years now, even before the old man had died. If she was to be kidnapped, it might force Ranson to change his mind about a lot of things; especially if the other were sweet on the girl, and Wilder thought that to be entirely possible. He kept the idea in the forefront of his mind. If Garvey and Wendell failed in their mission, it was something he had to fall back on.

*　*　*

Doc Fordham came out of the small cell for the second time that day, set down his bag on the desk in the sheriff's office, and lowered himself gratefully into the chair, taking out a thin, black cheroot and placing it carefully between his lips, rolling it around his mouth for a few moments as if savouring the firm feel of it before lighting it. Then he lit it and sat back in his chair, looking over the top of the desk at Chris.

'Well?' Chris asked. 'Do you reckon he's goin' to live?'

'He'll live,' stated the other, glancing down at the redly glowing tip of the cheroot. 'A slug in the shoulder never kills that kind. The devil looks after his own, they reckon, and I think that applies in his case. He'll be fit enough to be strung up when the time comes.'

'I'm glad to hear it.' Chris broke open the shotgun that lay on the desk and pushed the two large cartridges home, then closed the weapon with a snap that jarred loudly in the silence of the office.

Fordham noticed the other's action, gestured towards the shotgun with his left hand. 'You expectin' trouble?'

'I guess it's likely. Wilder will know about this by now, probably knew first thing this morning and he knows he's got to get Maxwell out of here before he talks and tells us a lot of things that he ought not to tell.'

'When do you reckon he'll come?'

'I don't think he'll ride into town and try to take him by force. There are too many people in town who know how Maxwell has been in cahoots with Wilder. If he's either shot down to stop him from talkin', or they try to bust him out of jail, they'll play it a subtle way, maybe try to make it look as though some of Diego's men have had a hand in it. That way, they'll kill two birds with one stone.' Chris's smile was cold, tight.

'You want me to stay with you? Two extra guns are better than none at all.'

'I don't reckon there's any reason why you should get mixed up in this,' Chris said quietly. He checked the chambers of the twin Colts, spinning the chambers quickly, then thrust the guns back into their holsters. Outside, the town seemed quiet. It was not late and he would have expected more activity on the streets, but it was as if the townsfolk had sensed that something was about to break loose at any moment, and they were keeping off the streets.

Getting to his feet, Chris walked to the door and opened it carefully before stepping through, standing a little to one side on the boardwalk, so that the light that streamed through the open door, spilling on to the dusty ground, was not directly at his back, silhouetting him there for any gunman to see and kill. The air that blew along the street, sighing down from the hills in the distance, was cool and pleasant on his face and in his nostrils. Tonight, the town was showing its quietest face for some time; yet for all of this comparative, apparent peace, he knew with a sudden certainty that it was merely an illusion, that there was danger out there in the dark-thrown shadows on either side of the street, danger that would come unexpectedly and from virtually any direction.

4

Night Hawks

The steak which Rosalie brought him from the hotel was tender and fried to perfection. She seated herself in the chair facing the long desk and watched him as he ate. Despite the tension in him, he worked his way through the meal with gusto, eating with relish. Seated in the chair by the door, tilting it back against the wall, Doc Fordham said harshly: 'You look worried, Chris. Expectin' more trouble?'

Chris glanced up from his plate, gave a brief nod. 'I'm always expectin' trouble in a town like this. Too quiet for my likin'. Besides, our friend Wilder won't be standin' still now that he knows we've got Maxwell locked up here in jail.'

'But we ain't sure that he does know,'

pointed out the other tersely.

'He knows, and he has to do somethin' about it — and soon. It's been quite a hectic two days. Another thing that worries me, is what Diego is goin' to do about this. So far, he hasn't put in an appearance and that surprises me.'

'Diego is a strange man. Maybe it's because he's a Mexican. Nobody knows which way he'll jump.'

'Eat up the supper I brought you and don't try crossing your bridges until you get to them,' said Rosalie quickly. 'Did you manage to get word to any of the other ranchers?' She glanced at the doctor as she spoke.

He pursed his lips, shrugged his shoulders a little. 'They were all for it,' he muttered. 'Some of 'em had heard about Brander and Maxwell. But they still weren't too sure about you, Chris. They figure that you might be forced to back down if Wilder decides to move in with all of his men and ride on the town.'

Chris pressed his lips tightly together, then drank down the scalding hot coffee. It was what he had expected. These men were not going to risk their lives, their ranches, everything they had built up over the years, just on the chance that he might be able to lead them against Wilder and possibly Diego. He pushed the empty plate into the middle of the table, fumbled for the makings of a smoke, then got to his feet and walked over to the window. Glancing out, he noticed that his mount was no longer standing at the hitching rail immediately outside. Puzzled, a tiny alarm bell ringing at the back of his mind, he motioned to Rosalie to put out the lamp, then opened the door, standing a little to one side before going out on to the wooden boardwalk, his right hand hovering close to the butt of the gun in its holster. The silence was enough to warn him that there was something wrong, very wrong. He had been too absorbed in his own thoughts to have noticed it before.

Narrowing his eyes, he glanced about him. His horse stood in the dust in the centre of the wide street, the reins trailing loosely on the ground. For a moment, he considered the possibility that the leather might have slipped, but he knew within himself that he had made the hitch properly, that it would not have been pulled loose by the horse.

'Get back inside the office,' he called as the girl made to come outside to join him.

He heard her step back into the room, then a swift movement at the edge of his vision caught his attention. The shadowed shape moved quickly across the face of the narrow alley on the far side of the street. There was the faint sound of boots in the muffling dust, then the brief, clearly-heard clatter of them as the man darted on to the boardwalk opposite him, running in a low crouch. The other darted across the beam of light from one of the windows and Chris caught a brief glimpse of a drawn gun. He let his gaze drift swiftly to either side, probing the shadows. There had to be another man somewhere around, with a gun lined up on him from the dark alleys.

Ducking back towards the barrel outside the sheriff's office, he threw himself down behind it, the Colts whispering from their holsters, his fingers bar-straight on the triggers. A couple of shots rang out from the far side of the street and he saw the bright lances of flame from the muzzles of the guns, pinpointing the hidden marksman. The slugs tore wood from the upright close by, went screaming off into the night, in murderous ricochet.

He snapped a quick shot at the gunman but it was impossible to tell if it had hit or missed its target. All the time, he felt the uneasiness in his mind as he tried to locate the second gunman. He had neither seen nor heard anything of this man but he knew with a strange certainty that this attack was following the classic pattern and the man across the street would never have given himself away like that if it hadn't been for the purpose of drawing attention to himself, while his companion moved into position.

'Better give up, Ranson,' yelled a harsh voice from the shadows on the other side of the street. 'We've got the place surrounded. If you turn Maxwell loose, we may consider letting you off with your life. If not, then we'll move in and make sure we finish you.'

Crouching down, keeping his head low, Chris waited, trying to get a clear glance of the other. There was a movement a little to one side of him and he half turned, then stopped as he recognised Doc Fordham's voice, yelling harshly from the window of the office.

'You got the rest of us to contend with,' he yelled, and punctuated his words with a sudden blast from one of the shotguns. The lethal hail of lead went bucketing across the street and

Chris was able to hear it quite clearly as it peppered the walls and uprights there, tearing through the wood, smashing one of the windows into a thousand pieces.

'Keep your head down,' roared Chris harshly. Although there was no light in the office window, he knew that the old doctor would make an excellent target for the bushwhacker directly across the street. Scarcely had the warning left his lips than there came another roar of sound, this time from the mouth of the narrow alley some twenty yards to his left. He narrowed his eyes, threw himself flat, then wriggled swiftly along the boardwalk, hugging the uprights, making as little noise as possible. Now that he knew the location of the other killer, it made things a little simpler. Pulling himself the full length of the walk, he slid snake-like over the dust, arms thrust out in front of him.

There was a wagon standing by the side of the street a few yards down from the office and he reached this in less than twenty seconds, swung up behind it and paused for a moment, waiting for the whining slug that would tell him he had been spotted by one of the others. But there was no sound from further along the street and he guessed they were still crouched in the shadows, looking for him. Bent slightly forward, he eased his way across the street, crouched down on the far side and balanced himself on the balls of his feet, eyes probing into the pitch blackness of the nearby alley. A moment later, his prying eyes had picked out the grey, blurred shape of the killer, his body pressed into the wall of the building that stood on the corner of the two streets, where they intersected.

'You heard what we said, Ranson?' yelled the man on the boardwalk. Chris listened to the voice carefully. He placed its source somewhere halfway along the front of the building and swung a little, waiting to see what the other man would do, letting the silence drag, finally growing weary of it, his finger itching on the trigger. As he waited, he remembered those two men who had been killed in the barn on the ranch and the wounded man he had somehow managed to get out of the blazing inferno before it had collapsed in ruins about him; and he felt the anger pour through him in a cold wave, chilling him. Patience made rock out of him so that he felt he could outwait these men no matter how long it took to break them down.

At last, he saw the man close to him begin to move forward, evidently not liking the stillness and silence at all. It was the sudden need to do something, to ease the tautness in his limbs which had prompted the killer to move; and he seemed to know that by doing so, he had given himself away, for he began to fire swiftly and with complete recklessness, raking the boardwalk in front of the sheriff's office with shots, clearly hoping that if he pumped in enough lead, some of it was bound to find its mark.

Chris stepped away from the wall, bringing up the guns as he did so. They bucked swiftly against his wrists as he sent two shots crashing into the darkness, saw the man stumble and give up a great shout as his legs went from under him, pitching him forward on to his face in the dust. His companion turned suddenly, began throwing lead. Chris heard the vicious hum of it close to his head and slugs struck the ground near his feet as he planted them wide. There was a part of a crowd on the street now, keeping in the background while the gunfight lasted.

Running forward, he reached the corner of the alley, pushed himself up right against the wall, keeping one eye on the man who lay face-downward in the dust, watching him closely for several seconds before he decided that there would be no more trouble from him. His breath quickened and drew deeper in his lungs as he pulled himself upright, then thrust his body forward, around the corner of the tall building. A slug blasted wood from the wall. Another missed his body by inches. But the gunslinger had given away his exact position and Chris pulled up his gun, pointed it at the place where the muzzle flash had lit up the boardwalk and fired. He heard the bullet smash through brick and wood, heard the other suddenly shift direction, knowing that he had been seen. Chris fired again. The bloom of the burned powder was blue-crimson in the pitch blackness and above the gun thunder, he heard the man cry out, his voice lifted in a shrill yell. Then the cry faded, the echoes of the gunshots drifted into silence around him and he heard the harsh, slow guttering of the man's breath as he lay flopped against one of the doorways.

Cautiously, his gun ready in his hand, Chris went forward, coldly and patiently waiting to put another shot into the man's body if he tried to move. But the other was finished, there was no more fight left in him, his body twisting and threshing slightly against the wooden uprights. From the other side of the street, Doc Fordham came forward, the shotgun hefted in his right hand, his face puckered a little as he hurried over. He stopped in front of the dying man, went down on one knee, laying the weapon down carefully, out of reach of the gunhawk.

Chris said: 'I aimed to kill him, Doc. He'd have shot one of us if I hadn't.'

The other nodded, turned and yelled at the small crowd in the street. 'One of you bring a light over here.'

A few moments later, one of the men shuffled forward, with a lantern in his hand. He stood on the boardwalk, holding it close to the man's body as the other bent to examine him. The gunslinger had been stirring slowly on the wooden slats, but now his body lay still and his breathing was so quiet that Chris had the feeling he was already dead, but after a few moments, he stirred and muttered something under his breath, the words so soft and slurred together that it was impossible for Chris to make them out.

'Must have cut across his lungs,' grunted Fordham. 'Nothin' I can do for him. He won't last long.'

'Reckon we ought to get him inside, Doc?' asked one of the men gruffly.

Doc Fordham shook his head. 'No need for that,' he muttered. 'He can die out here as well as in there.' It was a callous outlook, thought Chris, glancing sideways at the doctor, but he knew that it was not this that had prompted his answer. The man at his feet twisted a little, then his head dropped back on to the boardwalk with a faint thud and his breathing stopped with a long sigh that gushed out of him. Chris bent over the man, lifted his arm, felt the humped looseness of it and let it drop on the other's chest. He straightened, looked about him at the faces of the men clustered around the building.

'Anybody seen either of these killers before?' he asked harshly.

'Sure.' One of the men stepped forward, glanced down at both men, then nodded. 'I know 'em. Wendell and Garvey. They work for Wilder.'

'I figured that might be the way of it,' nodded Chris. He turned and made his way over to the office. He felt the hardness grow in him as he made his way along the narrow passage to the cells at the back, paused in front of the one which was occupied and stared through the bars at Maxwell. The other sat nursing his arm, glanced up with a faint grin on his fleshy features.

'Some shootin' out there, Ranson?' he asked innocently. 'Reckon the town ain't used to havin' you around.'

'Mebbe not,' muttered Chris. 'Seems Wilder must be plain scared at havin' you locked away in here. Sent along two of his hired killers to try to finish me and bust you out.'

Maxwell raised his brows at that, said nothing.

'Two fellas by the name of Wendell and Garvey. Could be that you knew 'em.'

'Never heard of either of 'em,'

protested the other mildly.

Chris shrugged. 'I wouldn't let that bother you none. They're both lyin' out there in the street. They ain't goin' to worry anybody now.'

For a moment, Chris felt sure that he saw the first faint flicker of doubt show on the other's fat face. Then it was gone as if it had never been, wiped away, and he was no longer sure that it had even been there.

'Reckon you'll be safe enough here until the circuit judge comes around. Then you'll stand your trial on as many charges as I can bring against you.'

'You'll never bring me to trial, Ranson, and you know it. If Wilder doesn't come ridin' in to get me out, Diego will. You can't fight the two of 'em, no matter how big you figure you are, or how many men you reckon you can count on from the other ranches or the town.'

'We'll see about that,' muttered Chris. Turning on his heel, he made his way back along the passage and into the outer office, lowering himself wearily into the chair behind the desk. Rosalie came over and stood with her hands resting on the top of the desk, looking down at him, a worried frown creasing her forehead.

'You're worried about Wilder, aren't you?' she murmured softly, glancing up as the outer door opened and Doc Fordham came in.'

'Not particularly Wilder. It's this *hombre* Diego I'm worried about at the moment, because I can guess pretty closely what Wilder's next move is goin' to be; but I know nothin' about Diego.'

'Then I reckon this is where you get the chance to find out about him,' said Fordham pointedly. 'He's ridin' along the street with a bunch of his men. Looks to me like there might be trouble.'

Chris heaved himself from his chair, walked quickly to the door and thrust it open, looking out into the shadowed street at the tightly-packed bunch of men who rode at a slow walk along the street. The group of riders halted in front of the sheriff's office and for a long moment, there was no movement. Chris was aware of the squat, dark-haired man who sat the large, black stallion, watching him from beneath the rim of the wide sombrero.

'Señor Ranson?' inquired the other, after a long pause, the flash of white teeth showing clearly in the shadow of his face.

'That's right,' said Chris clearly. 'And you must be Miguel Diego.'

'I am Diego.' Again the flash of a smile on the other's face. 'I wish to talk with you, Señor Ranson.'

'Better step down and come inside,' Chris said tightly. He threw a quick, sideways glance at the men the other had brought with him. Diego noticed this, and said something harshly in fluid Spanish. The men swung down from their saddles, hitched their mounts to the rail and then moved off in the direction of the nearby saloon. Diego waited until they had gone, then swung easily from the saddle, and came forward. 'Now we can talk alone, Señor Ranson,' he said smoothly, his dark eyes never once leaving Chris's face.

Chris stepped to one side, allowed the other to precede him, then closed the outer door. The Mexican glanced at Rosalie and Doc Fordham for a moment and some retort seemed to be balanced in his mind; then he shrugged his shoulders and walked over to the chair in front of the long desk, sat down in it and turned to face them.

'I have heard of the trouble there has been with Matthew Wilder,' he said softly, smiling broadly. 'I came into town to see if you needed any help. He is a very bad *hombre*, Señor. Very bad. He tries many times to take my ranch from me and it is only because I have many men with me, that he has not been able to do so. But he will try again, once he has taken your place from you.'

Chris squared round and looked across at him, eyes narrowed a little.

With the other's back to the light from the lantern on the table, he could make nothing of the Mexican's expression beyond the broad twist of his smile. 'Just what do you expect of me?' he asked suddenly.

'Nothing, Señor. You have very few men on the ranch who will back you in any fight against Wilder. He has many gunmen, thirty, perhaps forty. You will need men to ride with you and I have such men.'

'I see. So you're willin' to throw in your hand with me in an attempt to finish Wilder?' Chris pressed his lips tightly together. This was something he had not expected. But now that he came to look at things objectively, he ought to have figured that something like this might happen. Diego would want to get rid of Wilder by any means that he could, even if it meant throwing in his lot with him.

Diego spread his hands wide on top of the desk, leaning forward. 'I have heard that you have locked up Sheriff

Maxwell in the jail and you have taken his place. It is good that there should be law and order here, but so long as Wilder is alive, that cannot be. Believe me, Señor, I have lived here for many years and I know him. He is a man who desires power and wealth more than anything else in this world. He will kill for it, destroy for it.'

'And you — what do you expect to get out of it?' Chris grinned thinly. 'I don't suppose that you'll do this for nothin'.'

'But of course not. When this is finished, I shall take over Wilder's ranch. That is fair exchange, is it not?'

'Perhaps.' Chris nodded slowly. He was still unsure of the other. There was something in his story which did not ring quite true. He reckoned that Diego was more than capable of pitting one side against the other, standing in the background until the fighting was over and then stepping in and taking over all that was left, knowing that neither side had enough men to oppose him. 'I'll think it over,' he said finally.

The other gave him a studying glance and for a moment, the smile slipped and there was a hard tightness on his features. Then he shrugged negligently, took out a thin cheroot and lit it slowly. 'I would advise you not to wait too long, *amigo*. Matthew Wilder is a very impatient man and when he learns of the shooting tonight, he will seek revenge. Can you stop him if he rides into town, or against your ranch, with forty gunmen at his back?'

'I'll still think over your offer, Diego,' he said firmly. When the Mexican was gone, he leaned back in his chair and forced himself to relax, not aware until then that his body had been taut, every muscle pulled tight inside him.

'You're not goin' to trust that snake, are you?' muttered Doc Fordham, standing by the side of the desk, glancing down at him. 'He's only waitin' for you to move in on Wilder and you'll find that there'll be no men at your back. When you're all done, he'll move in and scoop the jackpot.'

'That possibility had occurred to me,' Chris murmured. He rolled himself a smoke and pulled the cigarette smoke down deep into his lungs. 'But can I afford not to take him up on his offer? He knows that he's got me in a cleft stick. He can always use his men to aid Wilder and there's no force in the whole State could stand up to both of 'em if they joined forces.'

Rosalie watched him, her face shadowed and soft. 'The ranchers will stand by you if you steer clear of Wilder and Diego,' she said, forcing conviction into her tone.

'Will they?' Chris shook his head slowly. 'Even if you're right, they don't have enough men among the lot of 'em to face up to Wilder and Diego. I reckon we have to accept Diego's offer of help. We've got no other choice.'

'If you do, none of the ranchers or the townfolk will lift a finger to help you,' warned the girl. 'I'm sure of that.'

Chris sighed, blew smoke into the

still air. He knew that the girl was right. He was supposed to represent law and order here in the town, and he could not do that if he allied himself with men such as Miguel Diego. There were several ways of enforcing law and order, but they did not include working hand in glove with killers, even if that seemed to be the only way left open to him.

'I reckon you'd better grab yourself some sleep,' broke in Fordham, changing the subject abruptly. 'You might be able to think things over a lot more clearly in the mornin'.'

'And Maxwell? What happens if Wilder decides to try again durin' the night?'

'I'll stand guard,' declared the other positively. 'There won't be any more trouble, but if it'll make you feel easier in your mind, I'll act as your night man. If there's any sign of trouble, I'll waken you.'

Chris wanted to protest, but he knew that at the moment, he needed sleep more than anything else and he was only too grateful to accept the other's offer. He finished his smoke, checked the twin Colts and the Winchester, took them with him into the back room and stretched himself out on the cold bed, the weapons close beside him, where he could reach them within seconds.

Outside, the town was quiet. The shooting had stirred it up a little, but it was not long before it had gone back to its usual stillness. Lying back, stretching himself out full length on the low bed, he closed his eyes and fell asleep almost at once.

★　★　★

Early the next morning, Matthew Wilder stood on the wide, back porch of the ranch house and watched the oncoming storm develop. It had begun as a high piling of the thunderheads over the distant mountains, the black masses of cloud building up from the horizon, dark and brooding, promising the threat of rain. He felt a responding tightness grow within him as he contemplated the news which had been brought to him two hours before, while it had been still dark, with only a thin, grey line showing where the dawn was about to break. The fact that Wendell and Garvey were dead, shot down by Ranson in the streets of town, scarcely affected him. Both men had clearly been fools, but they had claimed they would finish Ranson and he had been forced to let them have their chance, knowing only too well what the price would be if they failed.

But the additional item of news, namely that Diego had been to visit Ranson and the two had talked together in the sheriff's office for close on an hour that evening, had brought a sense of fear and apprehension to him, something he had not known for a long time now. If Diego had offered to throw in his lot with Ranson, and the latter had accepted that help, then he could see all of his dreams and carefully laid schemes coming to naught. There had to be something he could do, but until this storm blew itself out, he would be unable to ride out with any of his men and force a showdown.

The stillness that hung in the air had lasted for more than an hour now, while the thunderheads had increased their piled-up intensity, threatening and black. Then, the wind struck. It came suddenly and unexpectedly, whining over the smooth prairie at the rear of the ranch, flattening the grass and within moments, the rain came hard on its heels, wind-driven water that hammered at the roof of the porch over his head, searching out any unsuspected openings in it, pouring from the roof on to the ground around the house, flattening the mud, turning it into a quagmire, large puddles forming in it. The windows had been shuttered, but even so, they banged and crashed against the walls of the house as the wind caught at them, threatening to tear them from their hinges. All work on the ranch had stopped and the men were huddled in the comparative safety of the bunkhouse. Out on the hill, in the lee of the rounded promontory of ground, the cattle lowed in abject misery, their tails turned to the wind and rain as it blasted past them, showing no mercy to anything that stood in its way.

One of the men came over from the bunkhouse, feet splashing through the muddy puddles of the courtyard, a long poncho trailing down to his ankles and the tall, wide-brimmed hat already funnelling water down over his face. He paused in front of Wilder, lifting his face, the water streaming down it, his eyes narrowed to mere slits.

'Goin' to last most of the day, boss,' Matson said.

Wilder forced a curt nod. Impatience was riding him, but he tried not to show it in front of the other. 'We'll wait until it blows itself out and then get ready to ride,' he said sharply. 'How many men do we have here?'

For a second, there was surprise on

the other's coarse, bluff features. Then he caught the drift of the other's reasoning, and his thick lips split in a snarling grin. 'Enough to take Ranson,' he said harshly.

'And Diego too?' queried Wilder thinly. The colour of his face was stronger and more marked than usual and pride caused him to keep his worry hidden deep within him, his eyes half-shut as the wind howled around his tall body. He deliberately held himself erect.

'You figure that Diego may go in with Ranson?'

'Perhaps. We know they were seen talkin' together last night. They wouldn't be discussing anythin' else, now would they?'

'I guess not,' said the other, his voice spare and dry. 'But it ain't likely that Ranson will accept help given by Diego. He knows what sort of a man that Mex is by now.'

'If a man is in a tough spot, he'll take help from whatever quarter it's given,' said Wilder ironically. 'Honest people will always try to turn the devil against himself.'

Wilder said no more, but went inside, closing the door quickly behind him. A blast of cold air swept past him and caused the fire in the wide hearth in the parlour to blaze up with a sudden, renewed fury as the draught caught at it. As he went into the parlour, he caught a glimpse of his reflection in the long mirror that stood between two lamps, eyed it critically. He was tall and broad, but with the beginnings of a paunch that sagged over the belt around his middle. He had known that this was the first sign of his physical degeneration and tried to hide it by pulling himself in consciously.

Events along the forty-five years of his life had hardened him, had given him that cold assurance and arrogance which was obvious to all who met him; but he liked to look upon himself as a man with an acute perception, the ability to see where his destiny lay and to take all steps necessary to see that he attained it. He had built up one of the largest forces of men in the state, killers, cardsharps, men on the run from the law, offering them safety and sanctuary in return for their allegiance.

Thoughts of having all of his plans slip away from him, disturbed him more than he cared to admit and he shook out his tobacco pouch and sifted some of the long, fine strands on to a creased paper and rolled a smoke, running the tip of his tongue over the paper. Thrusting it between his lips, he struck a match and applied it to the tip of the cigarette, pulling the smoke deep into his lungs, forcing himself to think clearly, turning over the problem that faced him in his mind.

Outside, the storm was sending rain down fit to beat hell. He heard it slashing at the windows beyond the stout shutters and a few moments later, the thunder rolled like the beat of a vast drum, hammering across the heavens.

Sinking into one of the chairs, he

continued to smoke the cigarette, his thick, heavy brows bunched forward, drawn down tightly over his eyes, showing his displeasure. When he had first come to this place, the Civil War had just rolled over this land, leaving it stripped and bare, a place where little would grow and from which all of the beef had been taken to feed the hungry mouths of the fighting men. They had said that nothing would ever grow there again, that no one in his right mind would try to start a herd in this country. But he had seen the tremendous potential here and there had only been old Ranson there with the same vision as he had himself. At first, they had managed to survive side by side. There had been good summers and bad ones, when the drought had lain over the land and cattle had died in their hundreds, without water in their bellies, nor grass to feed them.

Somehow, he had managed to survive and his one aim in life had been to climb so far from that state of chaos that there would never be another period when he would have to fight to survive. The ruthlessness had been born in him then. But he had met his match when he had tried to go up against Jim Ranson. There had been a man as hard as he himself, a man who had refused to back down in spite of everything he had been able to do. But there had been the others, small men who had faced bad times and not been able to repay the mortgages on their ranches. He had frozen them out without any feelings at all, taken over their places and built up a position for himself in this territory. Now he was damned if he would let himself be driven out like those men by this young whelp, Ranson, even if the other had somehow managed to link up with Diego in an all-out attempt to drive him from the territory.

The anger that seized him, remained with him all of the morning, while the fierce storm raged outside, lightning forking the beserk heavens and thunder rumbling, primitive and raw, bucketing off in whiplike echoes over the plains to all of the far horizon. There was a savagery in the storm which found answer in Wilder's mind. And then, as suddenly as it had come, the storm broke, passed away to the east. Wilder moved out on to the porch, felt the returning coolness in the air and watched the dark clouds rolling away, leaving the sun shining brilliantly in the blue heavens.

He stood for a long moment, watching the steam rise from the wet ground, lifting in wavering streaks from the backs of the horses in the corral. Soon, he knew, the heat would return and they would begin to wish that another storm might rise over the mountains to bring rain and coolness into the parched ground.

Matson came out of the ranch house, stood beside him, looking off over the stretching plains, quartering the horizon with his eyes. He stood quite still for a long moment, then said gruffly, 'You still goin' ahead with your plan to finish Ranson?'

Wilder hesitated for a moment, then nodded his head. 'But I've been thinkin' things out and I reckon it would be just plain stupid to try to crowd him out right now.'

'Then you ain't ridin' into town with the boys?' There was surprise in the gunman's tone. He swung squarely on to Wilder, gazing at him with a wrinkled brow.

Wilder sighed and shook his head. 'That could be what Ranson is expectin' us to do,' he explained. 'And we might ride into town just to find that there was a trap laid for us.'

'Then why not ride for the Ranson spread? If Ranson is in town, lookin' after Maxwell, we could take the ranch and finish things that way.'

Wilder breathed heavily and gave the other a bitter, killing glance. 'I figure I should have shot him down in the saloon that day when I had the chance, but I never figured he'd give us this much trouble. I thought it would be easy to run him out of the territory.'

'I always said it was a mistake to ride on to the ranch and fire that barn. It only served to put his back up and now we've got a wildcat by the tail. He's already killed three of our best men and Maxwell is in jail, locked up in one of his own cells. He ain't any good to us there.'

'He never was any good anyway,' snapped the other thinly. The other made him feel sour and embittered. He drew his heavy lips back from his teeth. 'I want you to ride into town — find out all you can about this deal between Ranson and Diego. I want to know exactly what I'm lettin' myself in for when I do decide to ride.'

★ ★ ★

Sunlight filtered into the streets of the town, following swiftly in the wake of the storm that had swept over the area that morning. It touched the blistered paintwork of the stores and the hotel, fell on the steaming dust where all of the moisture that had fallen with the storm was being sucked avidly out of the ground by the heat. Doc Fordham made his way slowly along the boardwalk from the sheriff's office. Yawning, he stopped off at the small store, went into the tiny diner and ordered a late breakfast, eating it slowly. He had been on watch all night, while Chris Ranson had slept like a dead man. Nothing had happened, just as he had told the other, but perhaps, he reflected, there had always been the chance, and there was no sense in taking unnecessary risks as far as Wilder was concerned. That man was as tricky and as cunning as a desert coyote and would have to be watched every minute of the day and night. He drank his coffee black, hoping it would bring some of the life back into his weary bones. He was getting just a little too old for this sort of game, he decided, sitting up all night and then going back to his surgery, ready to tackle all of the many patients he had waiting for him. Swallowing the last morsel of food, he drew a cheroot from his pocket, lit it and sat back in his chair, relaxing. Chris Ranson had seemed a lot better for the long night's sleep and there had been no trouble so far. Maybe Wilder had realised that here was a man as good as his grandfather, a man who would never back down in the face of trouble, but would go forward and meet it halfway. Once Wilder got that through his thick skull, he might decide to leave well alone and things would return to what they had been when old Jim Ranson had been alive, keeping the peace in the territory. It had been an uneasy truce between the two feuding parties, that was true, but it had been a lasting one; and that was really all that mattered.

Outside, a dog lay in the dust, panting a little. He could make it out through the open doorway. It lay there for a long moment, then pulled itself up on to its haunches and dragged itself lazily out of the direct sunlight, moving back into the shadows. One solitary rider came into town. Fordham caught a brief glimpse of him as he rode slowly past the dusty, fly-speckled window. The man had the brim of his Stetson pulled well down over his face, his head hunched forward a little as he sat in the saddle so that it was impossible to see his face.

Tossing a couple of coins on to the table, Doc Fordham got slowly to his feet and walked out of the diner. He would have liked to stay there a lot longer, letting his weary bones relax, but he knew there were people waiting for him and he was not the sort of man to let things slide just because he had been awake for most of the night.

Pushing open the door of the surgery, he stepped inside, closed it behind him and threw a swift glance along the corridor. There was only one man waiting for him. He heaved a faintly audible sigh of relief. There was the chance that things might be easy for the rest of the morning. Usually, there were at least half a dozen patients waiting to be attended to. Going into the room, he pulled off his jacket, went over to the basin and poured the pitcher of water into it, then washed his face and hands, letting the cool water trickle down his neck. He rubbed himself dry with the rough towel, felt the blood begin to circulate in his veins. He needed to shave, but there was not time for that. Perhaps later in the afternoon, he might be able to find time in which to —

The door opened softly behind him and he whirled to find the man he had seen waiting in the corridor pushing his way into the room.

'I'll be with you in just a moment,' he said coldly. 'In the meantime, if you would care to wait outside, I'll call you when I'm ready to see you.'

'I think you'll see me now, Doctor,' said the other thinly. He closed and locked the door at his back and Fordham found himself looking down the barrel of the gun which the other held at his hip. The barrel was still, stone-steady, pointed at his chest. No use to gamble on the chance of bringing up his own gun from its holster, although for a moment, the thought lived in his mind. With an effort, he forced himself to relax and stand quite still.

'Damn it all,' he said harshly. 'Put that gun away.'

'Not until you've given me the answer to some questions.' muttered the other sharply. He moved closer, reached out and pulled the ancient Colt from Fordham's holster, thrusting it into his belt. 'Now sit down and don't try any tricks. I ain't got no real likin' for you and I won't think twice about using this gun.'

Fordham lowered himself into the nearby chair. Not once did he allow his gaze to wander from the other's face. He knew that he had seen this man before, but he couldn't place him. One of Diego's men — or one of Wilder's? It was difficult to tell. Either man would be wanting to know the answers to some questions before they committed themselves to any course of action that might mean using all of their men in one all-out effort.

'When did Diego and his men pull out last night?'

'Diego, I never saw that *hombre*. You know he won't ride into town openly like that and — ' The lash of the gun butt across the side of his head stopped any further flow of words, sent him reeling back in his chair, so that he half fell from it. Blood began to trickle down his cheek from the cut above his right eye and the searing pain of the blow lanced into his brain.

'Reckon you figure I'm playin' games with you, Doc,' grunted the other. His pale eyes snapped angrily. 'I happen to know that Diego came into town last night and that he rode across to the sheriff's office to have a parley with that *hombre* Ranson. I want to know what they talked about. Is Diego plannin' to link up with Ranson and the ranchers? When are they figurin' on doin' it, and how many men have they got at their backs?'

'If you know so much, then there ain't nothin' more I can tell you.' Somehow, Fordham got the words out through shaking lips. He knew that this man would kill him without any hesitation, whether he got the information he wanted or not. And he knew too, that this was one of Wilder's men, probably one of the Matson brothers he had heard about, men who rode with Wilder,

'There's plenty.' The other leaned forward, thrusting the muzzle of the gun hard into Fordham's stomach. The doctor winced as a further stab of pain went through him and sweat mingled with the blood that trickled down his face. He ran the tip of his tongue around his mouth, tasting blood. 'You goin' to tell me the easy way, Doc, or do I have to get rough?'

'All right, so Diego rode into town yesterday. He tried to get Ranson to go in with him, but he refused.'

Suspicion and disbelief flared in the other's eyes. 'You expectin' me to believe that Ranson refused Diego's offer of help, when he knows that without it he doesn't stand a chance in hell?'

'I reckon you don't know what kind of man Chris Ranson is. How could you? He's a man who believes in the law, a man who hates those outside the law, and that goes for Diego as well as you and the man you ride for.'

A sudden heat showed in Matson's face and for a moment, the pressure of the gun muzzle into Fordham's chest increased, forcing the other back into the chair until he could move back no further and the sweat popped out on his forehead and began to trickle down his face, twisted into a grimace of pain. Matson's lips were pulled back in a sneering grin. 'So Diego won't be ridin' with Ranson? Reckon that's all Wilder wants to know.' He got to his feet, thrust the gun back into his belt as if recognising that there was no danger from the doctor now. He made a gesture of impatience.

'Let's move,' he said sharply. 'Out the back way!'

'Where are we goin'?' asked Fordham harshly. He put up a hand and gingerly felt the wound on the side of his face.

Matson grinned widely. 'You don't reckon I'd be fool enough to leave you here to go runnin' across to that jumped-up sheriff, do you? We're goin' to have a talk with Wilder. Reckon he'll know what to do with you.'

He made Doc Fordham move ahead of him, through the store room at the back of the building and out into the narrow, rubbish-filled alley. A mangy cat ran howling from behind a pile of boxes, vanished along the alley at the far end. Where the alley linked up with the side street, there were two horses waiting. Fordham eyed them narrowly. It was clear that Matson had planned this well, had made sure of everything. He experienced a sinking feeling in the pit of his stomach as he swung himself up wearily into the saddle. Matson climbing up smoothly and easily on to the other horse, keeping a wary eye on him in case he tried to make a break for it.

Nodding curtly along the street, Matson indicated that the other was to ride in front of him. There were few folk about in the street and none of them paid the two men a second glance.

The first sun was high above the rocky shelves of the distant mountains as they headed out of town, but in the valley, the air was still cold and grey, still in shadow. Turning off the main trail, Matson led the way into the thick brush that grew along the side of the hill. The thick carpet of pine needles muffled the sound of hoofbeats and Fordham knew with a sick certainty that anyone on the trail would be unable to pick out the sound of their horses, even though they might be only a hundred yards or so away. The almost solid mat of interwoven branches over their heads trapped the sunlight, allowing little of it to filter through and they rode in a deep green silence which seemed to have been unaltered for a thousand years.

'I suppose you know that Ranson will come ridin' out after me as soon as he discovers I'm gone,' said Fordham softly, breaking the silence that had existed between them since they had left town.

Matson sneered. He pale stare sharpened. 'Maybe that's just what Wilder is hopin' he'll do,' he declared flatly.

Fordham eyed him steadily for a long moment as they rode along the narrow, twisting trail through the tall pines. Then he shook his head emphatically. 'If you're figurin' on getting him to ride into a trap, you're wrong. He's too smart for you, or Wilder.'

'If he's reckonin' on the ranchers ridin' with him, he's due for a big surprise and he'll soon find out he ain't quite as smart as he figures he is.'

5

Dawn Attack

The Wilder ranch, built against the lee of a small, smooth-rising hill, seemed on casual appraisal to be a single-storey affair, smaller than the Ranson place. Actually, at the rear, due to the slope of the hill, there was an additional section to the building, a sort of step-up, which Matthew Wilder used as a store room. Here it was that Doc Fordham found himself imprisoned after arriving at the ranch. They were taking no chances with him, had tied him tightly to the chair in which he sat, the thin ropes biting tightly and painfully into his arms and wrists. The knots had been tied by an expert and no matter how he twisted and struggled, it was impossible to loosen them at all. In the end, exhausted by his attempts to free himself, he sank back in the chair and tried to find a comfortable position, to relieve the agonising spasms of cramp which threatened to knot every muscle in his arms and legs.

The room was dull with dingy light and full of stale odours which assailed his nostrils and he made no effort to hide the grimace of distaste as the door opened and Wilder came in, followed by the two Matson brothers. They took up their position on either side of the door, leaning nonchalantly against the wall, grinning viciously as Wilder walked forward and stood to front of him, staring down out of bleak, cold eyes.

'I'm sorry it had to be like this, Fordham,' Wilder said. 'I hadn't meant that you should be brought here. All I wanted was information, but it seemed that you or Rosalie were the only ones who could supply that information, except for Ranson himself, of course, and it's not likely that he would have talked so easily. But you have to realise that we couldn't leave you in town, ready to run to Ranson and warn him of what had happened. You'll have to stay here as our — guest, until this little affair has all been sorted out.'

'Just what is it you're planning to do, Wilder? Take over the whole town just to bust that no-good Maxwell out of jail?'

'Maxwell!' Wilder grinned thinly. 'He means nothin' to me. He was just a fool to let himself get caught like that. Trouble is that we all seem to have figured this *hombre*, Ranson, wrong.'

'You reckoned he'd be easy to run out of the territory, like his father.' Fordham stared straight at the other, knew that he had touched a tender spot. 'I guess you'll find that you've underestimated him, and overplayed your hand this time; because he'll never stop until he's finished you for good.'

'Could be that he'll never have that chance,' said the other with a cold, calm assurance. 'I hear that he's trying to whip up the ranchers into getting their men behind him and run me out of the territory. Even now, he's in town, waitin' for me to ride in and force a showdown.'

Fordham nodded, but said nothing. For a moment, he struggled again against the ropes that held him, then gave up.

Wilder said tightly: 'We'll be leavin' you here in a little while, Doc. Come nightfall, we're ridin' out and headin' for the Ranson place. Reckon we can take it without any trouble while Ranson sits in town waitin' for us. When we don't show up, he might get around to thinkin' that maybe he's wrong and we ain't coming into town; but by that time, it'll be too late for him. With the Ranson spread in our hands, he won't stand a chance, even with the rest of the town behind him.'

Doc Fordham tightened his lips, glared up at the other, trying to keep the coldness in his chest from showing through on to his face. He knew that Chris had decided to stick around in town and wait for Wilder to show up there, that he had already decided to get the rest of the men from the ranch to ride out into town and meet him there and this would leave the ranch itself virtually unprotected. Somehow word had to be got to him to warn him of this new danger.

'Do I get somethin' to eat?' asked Fordham, playing for time. He had to get to know something more about Wilder's plans if he could, and he guessed that the other would not be averse to talking if he considered that there was no possibility of his prisoner getting away from this place in time to warn Chris.

Wilder considered that, then nodded, turned to one of the men at the door. 'Get him somethin' to eat,' he said tightly. 'Untie his hands, but keep his legs tied. When he's finished, be sure that you tie him up again.' Wilder stood eyeing the prisoner with a look of satisfaction and vicious, savage triumph. He had obviously not forgotten the humiliation he had suffered at the hands of Chris Ranson, the way his men had been shot down in front of many of the townsfolk, and now he was determined that this would not happen again, that he would have his revenge on the other, would show him who was the top man in this part of the territory,

Going over to the door, as one of the men slipped out, he said to the other: 'Get the rest of the boys rounded up. We're moving out tonight, and I reckon we ought to reach Ranson's spread by dawn. Then there'll be no trouble taking over the ranch.'

With food inside him and a smoke thrust between his lips, Fordham felt a bit better than before. The throbbing pain inside his head where the blood had crusted over the deep gash, had eased, allowing him to sit and think things out logically, but for a long while, there had seemed to be little profit in his thinking. Bitterly, he could only sit there, his hands free of the ropes while he finished the smoke, reflecting on how the cards were stacked against both himself and Chris Ranson. Maybe he ought to have chanced getting away from his captor while he had been in town. Now that he was here, there was little chance at all of getting to warn Chris Ranson in time. There was an inevitability about Wilder's plan that was almost frightening. His one hope was that he could outwit the man left to guard him once the others had ridden away. There was bound to be a spare horse around, and Wilder's evident assurance that everything would go his way, would mean that they would travel relatively slowly along the trail to the Ranson place. Wilder himself had maintained that they would not launch their attack on the ranch until dawn.

Outside the store room, there was the sound of heavy foot-steps coming closer and a moment later, the door was unlocked and one of the Matson brothers stepped inside. He eyed

Fordham casually from beneath lowered lids, clearly sure that there would be no danger from this old man.

He stood leaning against the wall for a moment, a sneering grin on his craggy features. Then he pushed himself upright, walked over to the chair, his eyes wary, and picked up the rope which had been used to tie Fordham's arms. 'Reckon it's time I made sure you're safely tied up,' he said harshly. 'The boss will be ridin' out soon with the rest of the boys and then there'll be just you and me here, so I figure we should make ourselves comfortable. You're goin' to be here for quite a while, at least until Wilder gets back with the news that he's taken the Ranson place. Then, maybe, he'll decide to let you know.'

Reaching forward, he wrapped the rope tightly around Fordham's arms and chest, pulling it more tightly than was necessary until the other groaned with pain.

'Reckon that ought to hold you,' he

said thinly. His big face twisted into a scowl. 'If you don't give me any trouble, you won't come to any harm.' He placed the lighted paraffin lamp on the table a few feet away, then went out of the room, closing and locking the heavy door behind him.

Fordham let his breath go in a long sigh, his gaze flicking around the room. The sense of urgency was rising in him, urging him to do something. He tested the ropes around his shoulders once more, but they had been tied as tightly as before and there was no way of loosening the knot. Exhausted, he sank back, feeling the sweat break out on his forehead and the palms of his hands. He did not doubt that without warning, Chris would stay in town and would lose the ranch to Wilder and his bunch. Outside, he guessed that the shadows were already beginning to lengthen. It was impossible to guess at the passage of time, but he had been questioned for more than an hour after arriving at the ranch and more than three hours

214

had passed since then. Besides, it was getting dark beyond the solitary window set in one wall. The lee of the hill would get the shadows first, he reasoned and that meant these men would be riding out soon, if they had not already gone.

Fordham's eyes were searching desperately now for some means of escape. He saw it at last, although he knew that it would mean taking a desperate risk. The lantern on the table was his only hope. Gritting his teeth, he began to move his bound legs, inching the chair over the rough floor towards the table. Pain jarred through his limbs, but somehow, he forced himself to keep moving, lips pressed tightly together to prevent any sound from escaping through his clenched teeth. He could hear nothing happening outside now and guessed that his jailer had decided to remain in the house, rather than in this room watching him.

The minutes slipped by and the

feeling of urgency in him grew. Once, the chair tilted under him, threatening to pitch him to the floor and he stopped his movements while the sweat spilled out of him. Thrusting his body and the chair forward, almost at the end of his strength, he finally reached the table, and steadied himself against it, the edge catching him across the chest. He felt his strength oozing away, felt the breath raw and harsh in his lungs and throat, but all the time, the knowledge of what would happen if Wilder managed to go through with his plans drove him on, gave him a strength that he had never known he possessed. Gasping air down into his heaving, tortured lungs, he forced himself to sit upright, thrusting down with his legs, straining against the ropes that bound him to the chair. The lantern was balanced near the edge of the table and he began to rock the long table back and forth, thankful for the bumpiness of the floor. The lantern began to shake, the glass rattling in its frame, the flame flickering as the oil began to slop around inside the metal container.

Gritting his teeth. Fordham continued to thrust against the heavy wooden table. He knew what the consequences of his action might be. If that oil were to run all over the floor once the lantern fell and if it were ignited by the flame, the whole room would become a blazing inferno within minutes. There would be little time in which he could cut himself free and get out.

He tried to lift himself even higher in the chair, but the ropes held him fast, made it almost impossible to move. Then the lantern tilted far over, slithered a few inches to the very edge of the table and went over, hitting the floor at his feet with a crash. There was the sudden flare of flame as the oil ignited. Without pausing to think, he thrust his bound feet forward, straining the ankles as far apart as possible, feeling the fire burn and singe the bottom of his trousers. Some part of his mind, detached from the rest, told him that he did not have a chance, that he would be burned before the ropes gave way. Sweat poured from his face as he held his feet there, tensing his muscles, ignoring the pain that lanced through his limbs. He tried to bend himself lower, twisting the cumbersome weight of the chair to one side as the fire started to catch at the table and the legs of the chair. His movements were awkward and the smell of smoke hit the back of his nostrils, bringing a rising nausea into his stomach. The ropes still held, binding his feet together, his ankles purple and swollen. Smoke drifted up from the floor of the room where the oil from the smashed lantern had run in a wide circle under the table. Fortunately, there had been only a small amount of oil in the lamp, otherwise the whole floor might have been a mass of flame by that time.

When it seemed that he could bear the pain no longer, he felt the frayed ropes begin to slacken their grip on his ankles and a moment later, with a wild, savage surge of strength, they snapped and he tottered shakily to his feet. There was a pounding agony in his forehead as the blood rushed to his head, but somehow he succeeded in remaining upright, backing away from the fire in the middle of the room, feeling the heat on his face, knowing that by now it had gained a firm hold there and within minutes it would have engulfed everything. Something glittered on the floor at his feet and he bent, managed to get a hold on it in his fingers and backed away into the corner of the room nearest the door, holding the fragment of sharp-edged glass from the lantern between his feet as he sawed at it with the rope binding his wrists. The rope which had held his arms to the sides of the chair had burned through in the flames which had leapt up the side of the chair.

His clothing was singed and smouldering, his lips drawn back over his teeth as the agony of singed flesh tore into his brain. Only the knowledge that he had to get away from this place enabled him to go on sawing the rope against the glass until the bonds fell away from his wrists. He rubbed them for a moment to restore the circulation, noticing the deep red marks where they had bitten deep into his flesh. Now there was no time to be lost. Snatching up the heavy wooden rod that lay propped in the corner, he commenced yelling at the top of his voice. Behind him, the fire was spreading rapidly through the room. If Matson didn't come running to see what was wrong, there was a good chance of him dying in this blaze before he had a chance of getting out.

Seconds later, however, there was the clatter of footsteps outside the door and Matson's harsh voice yelling: 'What the hell's goin' on in there, Fordham?'

'The lamp,' he yelled back. 'It fell from the table. Hurry, man! The whole place is burning.'

Some of the smoke must have been drifting under the door, confirming what he had said, for he heard the other mutter something savagely under his breath, then there came the metallic rattle of keys as the other fumbled for the one which fitted the lock. Tensing himself, ignoring the pain in his body, Fordham stood pressed against the wall beside the door, the heavy rod held high over his head. Swiftly, the door was thrust open. He caught a glimpse of Matson standing in the passage outside, staring into the room, open-mouthed and wide-eyed, peering at the blaze which was already beginning to lick up the far wall. The other gave a quick yell, started forward into the room, turning his head wildly from side to side. He sensed Fordham's presence there beside him, swung round, one hand clawing for the gun at his waist. But he was too late. It had still not cleared leather when the heavy weapon in Fordham's hands thudded with a sickening force against the back of his skull. Any lesser man might have died instantly under the crushing impact. As it was, Matson fell forward with scarcely a whimper, arms and legs folded under him. Swiftly, the doctor bent, hooked his hands under the other's armpits and hauled him outside into the corridor. Then, straightening up, he ran along the corridor, stumbling and falling, recovering his balance, running on until he was outside in the wide courtyard, sucking the clean, cold air down into his chest, feeling it like a soothing balm on his face and body. There had been nobody else in the house and he guessed that Wilder and his men had already ridden out. There was no telling how long he had to warn Ranson but he knew there was no time to wait and try to get his breath back. Every minute might be precious now.

There were three horses in the corral. They had obviously smelled the smoke which was drifting up from the back of the house and whinnied sharply as he moved over to the gate, pulled it open. It was hard work getting any of them to come to him, but finally, he succeeded in getting one of the saddles across one of the horses, tightening the cinch with hands that ached and burned. It took all of the strength that was left in him to haul himself up into the saddle, fingers scrabbling for the leather of the horn and clinging on with a desperate strength. The horse whinnied again, then plunged forward as he touched spurs to its flanks. The sudden jolt as it cleared the gate of the corral almost unseated him and he lay low in the saddle, clinging to the bucking animal with all the strength that was in him.

The horse veered sharply around the front of the house and pounded across the courtyard. Smoke, mingled here and there with licking tongues of flame, rose up from the rear of the building. Fordham thought for a moment of the man lying there outside that blazing room, but swiftly, he put the thought out of his mind. The other would have done exactly the same to him had the positions been reversed and at least, he had given the other a chance of life by pulling him out into the corridor where the through draught of air would keep the fire away from him for some time, until the rest of the building caught.

There was a grim sense of triumph in him as he rode away from the ranch. He did not doubt that Matson, when he did recover his senses, would catch one of the horses still in the corral and flee the area, rather than stay and try to put out the fire. By the time Wilder got back, if he ever did get back, he would find that he had no ranch to return to. It would be nothing more than a burnt-out, blackened shell.

The horse headed out over the desert trail while Fordham clung to the saddle tenaciously, giving the animal its head, not trying to rein it for the moment, trying to get his wind back, to clear his throbbing head. A whiplike branch of thorny mesquite struck savagely against his shoulder and twisted him in the saddle, almost throwing him. He tried to bend his head even lower but the long thorns raked the horse's flanks, sending it thundering forward, half-crazed by the pain, and lanced across his own exposed flesh. A wall of chapparal reared up in front of them. He could see no trail through it and the horse plunged onward without pausing, tossing its head, snorting, fighting, pawing at the dense mass of vegetation until it had somehow forced a way through. The long branches ripped and tore at Fordham's coat until it had been almost completely shredded on him. There was nothing he could possibly do now but try to dodge the upthrusting bushes, thorn and mesquite, that dotted the plains. Reeling weakly in the saddle, it was all that he could do to hold on as the animal twisted away instinctively from a patch of Spanish bayonet grass, avoiding the upthrusting needle-like points that reached for its legs and soft underbelly.

Ten minutes later, he felt consciousness begin to slip away from him. Somehow he managed to force himself up in the saddle, sucking air down into his lungs, fighting to clear his head, forcing his stultified vision to clear so that he could see where he was heading.

Only another quarter mile, he reckoned, and he would be out of this hell and on to the trail. He glimpsed it in the distance, winding away over the brown-and-green country, towards the low foothills in the distance which stood immediately outside the town. Once he reached them, he would feel comparatively safe. Then his nightmare journey would be almost over.

★   ★   ★

It was dark as Chris Ranson made his way across the wide street of town, with the cold night air beginning to flow down from the distant hills, striking into his body. Brow puckered in worried thought, he stamped into the sheriff's office and lowered himself into the chair behind the desk. Knowing that Doc Fordham needed his sleep after being on watch all night, he had delayed in going over to see him until mid-afternoon. When he had found that the other's place was empty and there was no sign of him, he had thought little of it at first. Knowing that as the only medical man in town, the other had plenty of work on his hands, he had figured that perhaps Fordham had been called out on an urgent case which had demanded instant attention. But when he had tried to find anybody who had seen the doctor since morning, it had become increasingly obvious that Fordham had left his office early that morning without bothering to get any sleep and had not been seen around since.

It wasn't like the other to ride out without telling someone where he was going, in case a patient needed him in a hurry and the more Chris thought it over in his mind, the more convinced he was that something was wrong. He glanced up as the door opened and Rosalie came in. Chris managed to dig up a weary smile. The sight of the girl was a heart-warming tonic.

'I've talked with some of the men who run the small ranches around town,' she said, a little breathlessly as if she had been hurrying. 'They're willing to throw in their men behind you if you decide to move against Wilder or Diego.'

'I'm glad to hear it.' He nodded slowly, thoughtfully. 'I didn't like the idea of accepting Diego's help, even to use it against a man like Matthew Wilder. But at the time when he made me the proposition, there didn't seem to be much alternative.'

The girl sat down in the chair facing him, eyeing him seriously. Then she said softly: 'You look troubled, Chris. Something on your mind?'

'Yes. I've been lookin' all over town for Doc. Nobody seems to have seen him since he left here first thing this mornin'. He called in at the store along the street and had a bite to eat, but that's the end of his trail. It ain't like him to go ridin' out of town without leavin' word with somebody.'

'You think something's happened to him?'

'I don't know. I only wish I knew where he was this minute.'

His head jerked up at the sound of a lone rider coming along the street outside. He had heard several riders head into town, but this one was different. This was somebody in a hurry, and acting on impulse, he pushed back his chair, got to his feet and crossed over to the street door, jerked it open and went out on to the boardwalk. The rider stopped in front of the office. For a moment, Chris peered out into the darkness, trying to make out the identity of the man who leaned forward in the saddle. The next moment he had moved quickly down the steps into the street and was reaching up to help Fordham from the saddle as the other sagged weakly to one side and would have fallen had he not been there.

Bending, Chris took the other's inert

body across his shoulders and carried him up on to the boardwalk and into the office, laying him down on the couch against the wall.

'It's Doctor Fordham,' said Rosalie quickly. She peered down over Chris's shoulder. 'Has he been hurt?'

Gently, Chris examined the barely conscious man, noticing the red marks on his wrists, others on his ankles and the burns which had blackened and scorched his clothing.

'He's been tied up somewhere, kept a prisoner,' he said thinly, rising to his feet and staring down at the other. 'Get me some hot water, Rosalie. I'll try to bring him round. I want to know what's been happening. I've an idea this is something important and the sooner I know about it, the better.'

The girl went through into the back room, came back in a few moments with a bowl of water and a towel. Pushing Chris to one side, she bathed the doctor's wounds, washing the blood from his forehead, exposing the deep gash just above the right eye.

'Whoever it was, they seem to have done their best to kill him,' she said, as she finished. 'I think he's coming round now.'

Chris went down on one knee beside the other, as the doctor stirred on the couch, his eyes flicking open. For a moment, he stared about him, with no sign of recognition in his eyes, then his gaze fell on Chris and the girl and a long sigh escaped him. He turned his head a little, his tongue flicking out, licking the dry lips. Chris went over to the desk, pulling the whiskey bottle from the drawer, filled a glass and brought it over, holding it to the other's lips. Most of the raw liquid dribbled down the other's chin, but he managed to get some of it down, coughing and gasping as it hit the back of his throat.

'Feelin' any better?' asked Chris quietly.

The other swallowed thickly, then nodded slowly, wincing as pain jarred through his head. He reached out and caught at Chris's sleeve with his right hand, fingers clawed into the cloth.

'Who did this?' Chris asked tensely. 'Take your time and lie still. You're safe now.'

'Wilder.' Fordham spoke thickly. 'He's ridin' out to the ranch with his men. He knows you're waitin' here in town for him and he figures he'll outsmart you.'

'You sure of this?' In spite of his concern for the other, there was a certain roughness in his voice. 'Was it Wilder who took you?'

'Matson. One of Wilder's men. They kept me tied up at the ranch after they'd questioned me about you and Diego. He was afraid that you might have thrown in with Diego, and if you had, he wouldn't have a chance of defeating both of you. Now that he knows you didn't, he's ridden out to the ranch. He's figuring on attacking it at dawn. You'll have to get your men together and ride out fast if you're goin' to stop him.'

Chris drew in a deep breath. So that was the plan. 'We'll stop 'em all right,' he said tightly. 'You'd better stay here with Rosalie. You'll be safe here.'

Fordham gave him a bright-sharp stare, then nodded weakly. 'Watch yourself, Chris,' he said warningly. 'Wilder has men in the hills, watching every trail, every move you make. He's no fool.'

'He's got to be stopped,' said Chris and there was ice in his tone. He lifted his glance to Rosalie. 'When can those men meet me at the edge of town?'

'Half an hour,' she said without hesitation. 'Most of them were friends of my father. They'll do this if I ask it of them.'

'Tell them to come ready to ride hard,' he said. 'I'll be waitin' for them at the edge of town.'

He walked over to the desk, picked up the heavy gunbelt that lay there and buckled it on. Strange, he mused worriedly, how it had now become a part of him. It felt as if he had been wearing these guns, ready to use them, all of his life, instead of just a handful of days. Was this how it got a man, turned him into a hardened killer? That was the fear which had always been in him. He had tried to stop from wearing guns, hoping that he would be able to take over the ranch and run it without having to resort to violence of any kind. But he had not been here very long before he had discovered, in no uncertain terms, that this just wasn't possible. If a man was not prepared to stand up and fight for what he had, then he would not last long in a place as lawless as this. Strength came only in the form of the sixgun, and the right of might was supreme.

Outside, he climbed wearily into the saddle, pushing all thought of what lay in front of him to the background of his mind. Overhead, the sky was bright with the brilliant powdering of stars and there was a round, yellow moon lifting clear of the eastern horizon, throwing long shadows over the quiet street. From the direction of the nearby saloon came the sound of a tinny piano and booming voices yelling out one of the marching songs of the war.

He rode past the lighted windows, past the narrow alleys whose black, empty mouths looked out into the street. The road was a solid streak of dust in front of him, touched with the pale moonlight which gave everything an eerie appearance. A horse stood sway-backed and sleepy in front of the hotel and near the outskirts of town, a couple of men sat on the boardwalk, staring in front of them, the tips of their cigarettes glowing redly, on and off, in the dark shadows as they smoked. Apart from them, and a drunk lying in one of the alleys, this part of town showed no life. The fact struck him forcibly and he fell to watching the side streets more closely. The thought of leaving Maxwell in the jail, unguarded, disturbed him anew; but in the circumstances, there was nothing else he could do.

It was almost thirty minutes later, before he heard the sound of riders approaching, some from the middle of the town, and others from the direction of the low hills which bordered it to the north. A moment later, they came in sight, two tightly-packed bunches of men, riding tall in the saddle, merging as they came up to him. Chris threw a quick glance over them, recognised one or two of the men as ranchers from the nearby hills. Paul Denver and Hank Rannigan, men who had came out here to settle this land with their families. Now they faced a common enemy and they had realised that there was only one way to destroy it, to make sure that it was finished for good; and that was to band together and ride with any man who would lead them. They had found this man in the grandson of Jim Ranson.

Rannigan said sharply: 'Rosalie said that Wilder was headed to your place, Ranson. You figuring on stopping him there?'

Chris gave a quick nod. 'I reckon we can get to the ranch as fast as they can if we take the mountain trail. They'll be headin' over the plains, takin' their time.'

'You got any men at the ranch?'

'A dozen. Not enough to hold off Wilder and his bunch for long, but maybe long enough for us to get there and take 'em from behind. They won't be expecting anythin' like that.'

'Sounds like a good plan,' agreed Denver. 'I like it. Whatever happens, we have to finish it soon. I reckon dawn is as good a time as any.' As he spoke, he wheeled his mount and rode up alongside Chris, his face hard in the moonlight which flooded the scene.

Chris gigged his mount, urged it forward. The rest fell in behind him, forming a long column, the mass of men beginning to shift and sway as they moved on out of town. Presently, the road turned upgrade, became rougher as they passed through a short belt of timber, on over the brow of a hill and up into the short switchback courses that led up and around the out-thrusting curve of the mountains, higher and higher, through belts of vegetation that shone silver in the drenching moonlight, then over belts of rough, open ground covered with rocks and thin scree. In places, the trail was little more than three feet wide and they were forced to ride in single file, walking their mounts. There would undoubtedly be some delay along this trail, Chris reasoned, and felt the urgency rise in him once again, riding him, forcing him to keep his mount moving more quickly than he really intended, for here the ground dropped away swiftly to one side, falling in a steep, sheer-sided precipice for many hundreds of feet down into the floor of the ravine.

The land was deceptive. In places, the trail ran along the edge of the chasm at a breakneck angle and his mount's feet slipped and slithered dangerously where he could no longer see the course in front of him. In the end, he was forced to cease pushing it to the limit, letting it find its own pace. It was a good horse and he had full confidence in it, but always, at the forefront of his mind, driving him on was the knowledge that with every minute that passed, Wilder and his men were drawing closer to the ranch, protected by only a handful of men who would certainly be taken by surprise.

It took them more than seven hours to clear the hills, to climb over the tall summits and down the other side, down fresh slides of earth where part of the trail had dropped away from the cliff face. By the time the grey band of light in the east began to dim the stars, they were riding across the smooth plains in the direction of the ranch, now less than three miles away. They had seen no sign of Wilder and his men, had heard nothing in the deep stillnesses on the mountain in the night. He had thought that they might possibly have picked out the sound of other riders in the distance, knowing how far such sound would travel at night under the cold, frost-sparkling stars and the fact that they had heard nothing worried him more than he cared to admit, even to himself. The other men kept up the punishing, breakneck speed, not hesitating to sacrifice their mounts to keep up with him, knowing what was uppermost in his mind. The trail ran across the river and they forded it without pausing, pulling up on the far side, water running from their horses. Gaining the shelter of the grove of trees on the other side, they slowed their mounts to walking pace. Now, they were almost within sight of the ranch and Chris held his breath until it hurt his lungs, sitting tall in the saddle, motioning the others into silence as he strained his ears to pick out the faintest sound. It scarcely seemed possible that they had succeeded in getting here before Wilder and his crew. They would have made good time over the plains, while they had been forced to pick their way carefully across the mountain trail.

'You hear them?' asked Rannigan tightly. He turned in the saddle to face Chris, features tight in the dim light.

'Nope. Don't hear a goddarned thing. They're probably down there right now, creeping up on the ranch.'

He dismounted, pulled the Winchester from its scabbard and moved up into the trees, waving the others to follow him. There was the soft murmur of the river in the near distance, but that was the only sound that disturbed the deep, clinging silence. Then, suddenly, sharply, shattering the quietness into a million shrieking fragments, sending the harsh echoes bouncing over the hills, came the report of a rifle from the direction of the ranch. Chris felt the sudden tightness in the pit of his stomach, knotting the muscles into a hard tautness. He pushed his way through the brush, ignoring the thorns that raked their needle-tipped fingers over his flesh. More firing broke out, the sound bucketing in every direction.

Swiftly, not turning his head, he waved the men behind him forward, dropped behind one of the smooth rocks as he peered down in the direction of the cluster of buildings in the low hollow. The flashes of muzzle fire were easily seen, and he saw that Wilder and his men had gained their positions all around the ranch, although the main concentration of fire seemed to be in the area of the corral.

Answering fire came from several of the windows of the ranch, and there were also some men holed up in the one barn that was still standing, not far from that which had been deliberately burned by Wilder's men some time before.

Every muscle in him was so tight that his whole body began to ache intolerably. He waited impatiently, until the men with him had spread themselves out, in a wide circle behind Wilder's crew. He did not want to tip his hand to the other until he was certain he had him just where he wanted him, with no possibility of escape. He already knew where Wilder had left his horses and he reckoned it would be possible to stampede them before any of the gunmen had a chance of reaching them and riding clear of the area.

The firing below had swung round as the gunhawks threw lead into the buildings. Dimly, Chris heard the sharp tinkle of splintered glass as one of the windows was caught by the blast and a man cried out in the overall dimness that lay over the scene. Time to be making his own play, he decided. A swift glance to right and left told him that Rannigan and Denver were in position with the rest of their men, just waiting for his signal to open fire. From their vantage points, they were able to look down and see most of Wilder's men stretched out on the ground near the barn or in the corral, where they were able to fire at the house without exposing themselves to the return fire.

He grinned viciously to himself for a brief moment as he realised how the tables would be turned in the next few moments, then sighted his Winchester on the dark shape that lay some fifty yards below him, his finger taking up the slack on the trigger. Before he squeezed it, he yelled loudly: 'All right, Wilder! Tell your men to get to their feet and throw down their weapons. We've got a bead on the lot of you.'

For a long moment, there was no movement at all from any of the men down below them. Then he saw several of them squirm around, bringing their guns to bear on any targets they could see behind them. Pulling back his lips, Chris squeezed the trigger and saw the man in his sights, suddenly jump and then flop back as the bullet found its mark. As if it had been the prelude to an overture of utter destruction, the entire hillside racketed with volley after volley of gunfire. The thing was terrible. Lead flailed through the air from more than a score of points all around the house and outbuildings. He heard more of Wilder's men shout and drop as they were caught in the withering crossfire that tore into them, cutting them down as they tried desperately to get to their feet and run for the horses. Chris drew back and away, pulled himself forward, down the slope, to the point where Wilder's mounts were tethered. Two men came blundering forward from the direction of the ranch as he rose up from the thin brush and moved in. Both saw him at the same instant.

He heard one of them yell something to the other, saw their hands come up, clutching their weapons. His own hands scarcely seemed to move, but in an instant, the twin Colts were in his fists and the two shots sounded as one. Both men staggered as the hot lead tore into them, remained poised upright for a few tense seconds and then tottered forward on the toes of their feet before pitching down in front of the frightened horses. Running forward, Chris loosened the reins which tethered them to the branches of the low trees, fired his Colt three times into the air, yelling at the top of his voice. Madly, the horses panicked, rearing and plunging as they stampeded into the distance.

The shouting and yelling went on, running at random around the buildings. In the grey dawn, it reminded Chris of nothing so much as the continual howl of a racing wolf pack. Firing continued to break out, first at one spot and then another as Rannigan and his men moved in for the kill. A man came running out of the dimness directly in front of Chris, crouching low, firing as he ran. Chris felt the passage of hot lead past his face, heard it strike the rocks near him and ricochet into the distance with the whine of tortured metal. Chris snapped a shot at him, saw the other swerve. It was impossible to tell if the slug had hit or not. The man went down behind one of the rocks, remained out of sight.

Slipping to one side, Chris came up against Denver, said harshly: 'Where is Wilder?'

The rancher shook his head. 'Haven't

seen him since we got here. Reckon he must be down there somewhere.'

'Keep up your fire. I'm goin' down to look for him. I don't want him to slip through our fingers this time and in all this ruckus he's liable to do just that.'

He crept to the edge of the trees, stopped to listen to the firing, judging its position and intensity before moving on. Most of the men inside the ranch house were firing now, their fire cutting into Wilder's men as they floundered in the grey dimness, striving to get away from the terrible crossfire that grew in intensity, cutting them down as they ran headlong for cover which no longer seemed to exist for them.

Chris let his breath fall away, then rush into his lungs, only to exhale it again as he plunged down the slope, heedless of the slugs that tore through the air around his body. Reaching the side of the long barn, he paused, looked about him through narrowed eyes. Most of the gunhawks had moved well away from the house and were trying to escape into the hills. Leaderless now, they ran in little groups, seeking to get away, but running into Rannigan and his men on the lower slopes of the hills.

Carefully, Chris edged around the edge of the barn, then paused suddenly. A familiar voice out of the dark opening where he had expected to find no one but perhaps a few of his own men, said sharply: 'Let that gun drop, Ranson. I've got a bead on you and I'm just itchin' to pull this trigger. But I want you to see who's sendin' you into eternity.'

Chris turned slowly. Matthew Wilder was standing with his back to the wall. There was a tight expression of triumph on his fleshy face, his teeth showing in a snarl, his deep-socketed eyes glowing in the dim light. The air here was thick and heavy with the smell of gun smoke.

'Don't try to be a hero, Ranson. Maybe you've killed most of my men, but I'll see that you don't live to get anythin' out of it.'

For a moment, the thought lived in

Chris's mind that he might be able to swing and beat the other to the shot, but one quick look at Wilder was enough to tell him that to try such a move would be utter suicide. There was a cold glitter in the deep-set eyes. Chris saw the hammer lift on the other's gun. The round black hole of the muzzle was pointing directly at the middle of his body. He reckoned he had only a second or so to go.

Back in his head was the knowledge that he had been badly caught off guard by the other. He ought to have known that Wilder would have stayed around, hoping to get a shot at the man who had engineered all of this, destroyed his force. Even the remnants of Wilder's outfit would never ride solid behind him again unless he at last brought some kind of order out of this chaos and destroyed the man who had been responsible for it.

All of these thoughts raced through Chris's mind in the split second that he stood there, the Colt beginning to slip from his fingers at the other's sharp command. He knew that Wilder expected him to try to make a fight of it, even at that last moment, but he did the one thing that the other did not expect. He dropped, a split second before the gun roared in Wilder's fist, and lunged forward with his shoulder as he went down. The lead whined an inch over his head and smashed against the upright of the door. Wood splintered on Chris as he hit Wilder's feet, throwing him back against the wall. A loud gasp came from the other's lips as his head struck the thick timber with a sickening crack. Savagely, Wilder tried to twist away, to bring up his gun again. Chris had released his hold on his own weapon the moment he had hit the ground. Now he grabbed at Wilder's wrist, thrusting it away as the man heaved with all of his strength, trying to twist the gun so that the muzzle pointed at Chris's head. Another shot bucketed out as Wilder pressed the trigger, but the bullet went high.

Smashing down with the side of his hand, Chris knocked the gun from the other man's fingers, sent it hurtling into the dirt. Wilder uttered a choked cry, then his hands clawed up at Chris's throat, getting a throttling grip. The strength in those long talons of fingers shocked Chris. He could begin to feel the effect of the strangling fingers as the other tried to heave himself upright and his eyeballs bulged as if they would jump from their sockets. The pain was making him dizzy and there was a roaring in his ears that drowned out every other sound, the constricting band of agony around his chest growing tighter with every passing second as his lungs were starved of air. He knew that he had to break the other's hold soon or die. With a surging effort, he got both arms free and slammed them against the side of Wilder's head. The man gurgled in pain and the grip on Chris's throat slackened fleetingly. In that second, he jerked his head back, feeling the nails tear at his flesh. The other's grip did not loosen completely, but his head and shoulders were lifted clear of the ground by the sudden movement. Chris seized his chance, thrust forward with his own head and a groan was forced from Wilder's lips as his skull crashed against the hard ground under him. Tearing his bruised throat free of the other's hands, Chris swung his fist, sending it crashing against Wilder's unprotected jaw and the man, with a pulping groan, went limp. Sucking air down into his tortured lungs, Chris managed to get to his feet, stood swaying as he stared down at the other through tear-blurred eyes. Wilder lay where he had fallen for several seconds, then shook his head as if to clear it and tried to push himself on to his hands and knees, head hanging down between his arms. All of the fight seemed to have been hammered out of him. Then he moved forward in the direction of Chris's gun, lying in the dirt a couple of feet away. One hand reached out, clawing for the weapon. He scarcely seemed to know what he was doing, or of Chris's presence there. Almost, he had his fingers curled about it. Then he collapsed on to the ground as Chris kicked him in the head and stood back, drawing himself upright. There was the pounding of feet in the near distance and a moment later, Denver came running around the corner of the barn, his drawn gun wavering a little as he sighted the two men.

'Hold your trigger,' Chris said sharply. 'I reckon he's finished.'

'Wilder?' asked the other tightly.

Chris nodded. 'He tried to bush-whack me from inside the barn. Would have done it, too, if he hadn't been too sure of himself.'

'The rest of his outfit are finished too,' grunted the other, thrusting the Colt back into its holster. 'The boys are rounding up any strays who might be tryin' to work their way through the trees.'

Chris nodded, picked up his gun and slipped it into leather. 'We'll take him back into town with us,' he muttered, jerking a thumb at the unconscious man lying at his feet. 'I reckon we can always find a rope to hang him once the judge has passed sentence.' He rubbed his throat tenderly with his fingertips, found it hard to swallow.

'I reckon this is somethin' that Wilder never expected,' grinned the other man. 'He must've figured it would be the easiest thing in the world to take your ranch, imaginin' you were more'n thirty miles away in town.'

'Thanks to Doc Fordham,' said Chris solemnly. He wondered how the old doctor was and a twinge of conscience touched him. True they had taken care of Wilder, and he would bother them no more. His men, what few of them were still alive, were scattered to hell and beyond, leaderless, representing no further danger to the territory; but Diego was still around some place, a man of a different calibre to Matthew Wilder, and possibly twice as dangerous. What was the Mexican doing now, while the town was unguarded? The thought troubled him, made impatience grow in him, but he knew that these men who had ridden with him were saddle weary and some of them had been hurt.

'Better get the men together and we'll have a bite to eat, and rest up the horses before we ride on back into town,' he said. The sun was just beginning to lift, colouring the sky a deep crimson in the east.

Denver glanced at him curiously. 'You ain't reckonin' on more trouble, are you?' he asked pointedly.

Chris drew in a short, swift breath. He looked closely at the other, trying to sort out the immediate things in his mind. 'I'm not sure,' he murmured finally, as they turned towards the house. 'Diego is still around and he wanted as much as Wilder did, but maybe he has a more subtle way of goin' about it.'

'Diego!' Denver gave him a sideways glance. 'Certainly he and Wilder were at loggerheads. Both wanted this spread when your grandfather died and as you say, Diego is a ruthless killer, maybe more dangerous than Wilder. He's like a rattler, coiled and ready to strike when you least expect it.'

'How many men has Diego got behind him?'

'Thirty maybe. Not as many as Wilder. And when he knows that Wilder is finished, he may think twice about tryin' to fight. He may back down rather than risk the same thing happenin' to him. He's no fool and it could be that he'll be content with what he's got, rather than lose everythin'.'

'Maybe.' There was little conviction in Chris's voice. He led the way into the house, turned for a moment and watched the rest of the men straggling in from the low hills and around the corral, saw them make their way over to the bunkhouse. He reckoned they would be ready to ride again at high noon. There would not be as many of them as had ridden out with him during the night. Some had been killed, others wounded. But would they be enough to stop Diego? He knew he would never feel easy in his mind until Diego was finished too, as Wilder was finished.

When high noon came, with the burning heat of the sun lying over everything, they rode out of the ranch and headed for the trail over the plain, back towards town. As he rode, Chris felt a sense of growing alertness in him, something which overrode the weariness that was deep inside him. The trail ran dog-leg fashion through clumps of cactus and mesquite, then out on to the broad, stretching plain which lay between the town and the ranch, with only the river to break the flat monotony of it. The sun pressed on them with a heavy, oppressive heat that burned through their clothing, and the harsh light flashed off the metal of their bridles with painful stabs of light. Dust was a silver screen all about them, hazing the men who rode with him and heat rolled back from the punished earth on either side of the trail, making a thin, unseen turbulence all about them, rising up and touching the shimmering hills in the distance, where they rose in great, undulant shapes on the skyline. The smell of the day was a burnt-out scent of dried grass and sage and the bitter alkali smell of the dust that was everywhere.

By the time they came within sight of the town, the middle-down sun was a glaring disc that shone directly into their eyes, even under the lowered brims of their hats and the horizons were burned a deep blue-yellow. Nothing had relieved the piled-up intensity of the heat and the day's ride had been a punishment for all of the riders and their mounts. Caked with dust and sweat, every breath was a labour, a tightness in their chests which turned them nervous.

A little before five o'clock, they

crossed the narrow bench of land that fronted the town and rode into the wide street. The town was quiet and as he turned his gaze from one side to the other, Chris felt a little of the nervous tightness draw out of him and he relaxed his tight-fisted grip on the reins.

Drawing rein in front of the sheriff's office, he slipped from the saddle and went inside, heels rapping a hollow tattoo on the boardwalk. The outer office was empty and there was a stillness there that he didn't like, a waiting silence that ate at his nerves. Stepping through the far door, he made his way along the passage to the cells.

For a moment, he paused in front of that which had held Maxwell when he had left town the previous night. Then with a muttered curse, he ran back into the outer office for the keys, saw in a single, sweeping glance that the rack was empty, ran back to the cell and blasted the lock into jangled ruin with a single shot. Thrusting the door open, he knelt beside the bound and gagged figure that lay on the low bunk, ripped the gag from the man's face and found himself staring down into Doc Fordham's weather-beaten features.

6

Long Vengeance

It took Chris only a minute's examination to determine that the doctor had been merely knocked out and then bound and gagged. The wound on the side of his head had been reopened and had bled a lot while he had been lying there and he groaned in deep agony as he stirred and came round. There was the clatter of feet in the corridor outside and Denver came running into the cell, taking in everything in a single glance.

Chris bit back a curse as he stared at the grey-haired rancher. 'I knew it was a mistake to ride out and leave this place unguarded, but I never figured that Maxwell would be able to trick Fordham into anythin' like this. He must've feigned illness and got the doc to go into the cell and then knocked him cold. But where's Rosalie? She should have been here.'

'Could be that she went for help,' suggested the other. He bent beside the doctor. 'He may be able to tell us when he comes round fully.'

Fordham muttered something under his breath, his head twisting from one side to the other, lips drawn back over his teeth. Then his eyes flicked open. For a long moment, he stared up at Chris and Denver, his gaze devoid of all expression.

'You'll be all right, Doc,' said Denver quietly. 'Just lie there and try to tell us what happened. Where's Maxwell? Did he make a break for it?'

Fordham swallowed thickly, then shook his head, wincing as the movement sent pain jarring through it. With a tremendous effort, he forced himself into a sitting position in spite of Chris's move to restrain him. Reaching out, he caught the other's arm, his fingers biting in with a steel-like, urgent strength. 'Diego!' he mumbled. 'I blame myself for this, Chris. I should've known that double-crossin' Mexican might try somethin' while you were out of town.'

'Diego!' Chris stared at the other in sudden shocked surprise. He felt the coldness draw tight within him.

'What time is it?' grunted the doctor, ignoring the other's sudden exclamation.

'Nearly five-thirty,' muttered Denver. 'We caught up with Wilder and brought him back to town for trial.'

'Where is Diego now?' asked Chris sharply. 'Did he come here just to bust Maxwell out of jail?' Deep inside, he knew that this had not been the case, but he had to live with that single hope for as long as he could, afraid of what he might hear from the other's lips.

'Maxwell?' Fordham shook his head. 'Diego claimed you'd run into an ambush, that you needed help and I was to try to get some of the townsfolk to ride out with me. No sooner had I turned towards the door than a gun was jabbed into my back. They pushed me into this cell after they'd turned Maxwell loose. Then they grabbed Rosalie and said . . . ' He broke off suddenly, as if unable to continue.

'Go on,' said Chris demandingly, the sudden fear crystallising into a deep conviction inside him. 'What about Rosalie?'

'Better give him time,' said Denver quietly, forcing Chris's grip on the old doctor's arm to relax. 'He's come through hell and it won't be easy for him to — '

'But don't you understand?' Chris turned on him almost savagely. 'Diego must have taken Rosalie with him when he rode out of town with Maxwell.'

He turned back to Fordham, saw the slight, almost imperceptible nod of the man's head. 'That's what they did all right,' grunted the other. He tightened his lips. 'Diego said that you'd get her back only when you signed the ranch over to him and rode out of the territory.'

Grim faced, Chris got to his feet,

sucked in a deep breath, his eyes very hard and still, pinched down as he looked across at Denver. He caught the rancher's steely look and jerked his head towards the door. Denver nodded, stepped out into the corridor and moved back into the outer office.

'Get some of your men to help Doc,' said Chris tightly. He took the Colts from their holsters, one by one, loaded shells into the empty chambers, then pushed them back into place. Denver looked sharply at him.

'You're goin' after them, despite the fact that you don't even know which way they're headed?'

Chris's jaw muscles bunched and his eyes flashed in swift, sudden anger. 'You know damned well that question don't need any answer.'

The other shrugged his shoulders swiftly. 'Only wanted to know,' he grunted. 'I'm comin' with you. Rosalie's father was a friend of mine. I can get more than fifty men who'll ride with us and — '

'No,' Chris snapped, tight-lipped. 'This has to be handled by me alone. A whole bunch of men on the trail will be spotted at once and I know enough about Diego to know that he'll kill the girl rather than let us get our hands to her again. He's got nothin' to lose in this affair.'

'Then I'll ride with you alone.'

'Two of us might be one too many,' said Chris, 'but thanks for the offer. I know how you must feel.'

Denver ran a hand across his mouth, brow drawn deep in thought. 'Somethin' you forget, Chris,' he said slowly, evenly. 'I know this country far better than you do. I know Diego too, know how his mind works. And I figure that I can read a trail as well as any man in these parts. Besides, we don't know how many men he has ridin' with him. I figure he won't have many. He'll need most of 'em to watch his own spread, knowing that when this is discovered, we'll ride against him, no matter what you plan on doin'. But if he was to head for the mesas to the south, there are plenty of places where they could hide out and hold off an army of men, just the two of 'em.'

'Then you reckon that Maxwell is ridin' with him?'

'Could be,' mused the other. 'Maxwell will be lookin' after his own skin now. He knows that if we get him and bring him back here, he'll stand trial, so he'll stick with Diego.'

Chris stared levelly at the rancher, then gave a brief, terse nod. 'All right. We'd better get started. There's no way of tellin' when they did this and the trail is goin' to get pretty cold durin' the night.'

Denver swung away. 'I'll get us a couple of fresh broncs,' he said harshly, then paused: 'Just one thing, Chris. When we do finally catch up with Diego and Maxwell and get a chance to nail 'em without endangerin' the girl, that's what we do?'

Chris's lips were drawn back into a thin, compressed line. 'I don't trust that

Mexican one little bit,' he said coldly, keeping his anger under tight, rigid control. 'He'll kill the girl rather than hand her over to us, whether I agree to sign over the ranch to him or not. He knows that I won't stop until I've destroyed him.' Unconsciously almost, his right hand dropped to the gun butt in his belt, fingers touching the smooth wood. 'When we get them, we drop them any way we can. We shoot them in the back or through the head, without any warnin' at all. Just one thing though, Denver.'

The rancher paused with his hand on the handle of the door, stared across at Chris with quizzically-lifted brows. When he finally spoke, Chris's tone was soft and filled with menace. 'When we finally locate 'em — Diego is mine.'

★　★　★

One last wave of red sunlight washed over the high hills, breaking into the deep purple of twilight, and then it was gone and darkness descended swiftly on the land. The pines which massed on the higher reaches of the hills stood in deep shadow as they thrust themselves up, tall and straight, arrowing towards the heavens. Here the air was thin and clear and cool on Rosalie's face as she sat high in the saddle, her gaze flicking from Diego's dark, swarthy features, to the sagging cheeks of the man who had once been sheriff, before he had been tossed into jail by Chris Ranson. The thought of Chris stirred some emotion deep in her mind and she fell to wondering what he would do once he rode back into town and discovered what had happened.

Would he guess where these men were taking her — or would he do as Diego had said and sign the ranch over to the Mexican in return for her life? Diego had wasted no time in making his move, once Chris and the others had ridden out of town to hunt down Matthew Wilder and his gunmen. He must have been planning this for some time, perhaps even when he had gone to Chris and offered to throw in his men, to help him against Wilder.

Diego's voice broke in on her thoughts: 'We should reach the mesas by dawn if we ride all night.'

'Don't you reckon we can rest up somewhere?' muttered Maxwell sullenly. 'These horses are mighty tired and there ain't much chance of anybody ridin' after us.' He seemed anxious and nervous, the sort of man who was eager to make sure of this chore, hoping that it would go off without a hitch, knowing Diego's reputation as a gunman and killer, but also unsure of what Chris Ranson, who had also shown himself to be something of a gunfighter, meant to do.

'Why don't you relax, *amigo*,' said Diego harshly. 'We've covered our trail pretty well and it's goin' to be dark within minutes. Besides, Ranson knows nothin' of this part of the territory.'

'Some of the others with him may,' put in Maxwell, unconvinced.

'Ranson won't follow us, you gosh-darned fool,' Diego hissed. 'He's got more sense than that. He knows he'll never get the girl back alive if he tries to track us down.' He sat his saddle squarely, cuffed his hat back on to the dark, curly hair and then tilted his head back, looking at the towering range that rose up in front of them.

'Heavy timber,' grunted Maxwell thickly. 'That will slow us down a lot.'

'It'll do the same for them, *amigo*,' said Diego thinly. 'And if they were to follow us and tried to work their way around it, they'd lose many hours before they hit the trail again.'

While the two men were eyeing the pines which rose in ordered array above them, Rosalie pulled the silk handkerchief from her pocket, bent low in the saddle, keeping her gaze on the two men as she let it drop among the rocks on the edge of the trail. This done, she urged her mount forward until she was level with the others. Neither man glanced behind her and in the darkness, the tiny square of silk would have been difficult to pick out from the boulders, but she could only hope that if Chris was following, that if he had, somehow, picked up the trail further back, he might spot it and know that he was moving in the right direction; for once up there among those tall pines, it would be virtually impossible for anyone but an Indian scout to follow them.

'All right,' said Diego thinly. 'Let's get moving.' He looked anxiously at the shadowed bank of the low foothills to either side, then urged his mount forward, with the girl behind him and Maxwell bringing up the rear.

★ ★ ★

Once they were well clear of the town, Denver slowed his mount, moved forward with an undue care, eyes scanning the ground in front of him, flicking from side to side, missing nothing. It was still sufficiently light for them to make out most of the details of the ground. They had crossed the wide river ten minutes before and Denver had spent several minutes walking his mount up and down the bank before pausing and pointing in satisfaction. The prints of three horses were just visible in the soft ground. There were also the scratches of a branch in the dirt and a few crushed leaves which told of the attempt which had been made by someone to obliterate the trail.

'I reckon they didn't make a good job of it,' Chris said tightly. 'Leavin' those leaves behind is a give-away. Ain't no branches near here.'

Catching up the reins, he urged his mount forward. Denver rode up beside him, his face tight and grim in the fading light. He stared directly ahead of him, up at the great, brooding weight of the mountains that lifted in front of the sunset. Only the expression on his face gave any indication of the thoughts that were running through his mind at that moment; but Chris could guess at them, the same thing had occurred to him. Once Diego got into the mountains, into the dense pines which covered the lowermost slopes, they would find it difficult, if not quite impossible, to trail him. All they knew at the moment was that three riders had passed this way recently. Everything pointed to it having been Diego and Maxwell, taking the girl with them, but if they were on a wild goose chase . . .

He let the idea drift swiftly out of his mind. It was no good thinking along those lines. They had to keep on following this trail in the hope that, at some time, the girl managed to leave some sign behind while the others were not watching, which would confirm for them that they were following the right trail and not riding in the opposite direction. Certainly Denver's idea that the Mexican was heading for the rising spires of the hills, seemed plausible. Any other trail would have merely taken him through low foothills, or out on to the stretching plain, and there would be little or no cover there where they could hole up with the girl. He fell to wondering, as he rode, how Diego intended to get word through to him to sign over the ranch. It would all have to be done legally, otherwise Diego would have no claim to it. It was more than likely that he would take Maxwell and Rosalie up into the mountains some-where and leave the crooked sheriff to watch the girl while he rode back into town, knowing that Chris dared do nothing so long as he had the girl well hidden.

Darkness came down swiftly as they rode on, eyes continuing to search the ground. There was a winding trail that led up into the foothills, the only trail they saw, and it was unlikely that Diego would be foolish enough as to try to force his way over unbroken ground, thereby slowing himself up more than was necessary. The cliff face was rock and earth, a very thin skim of earth which grew little here except for rough patches of coarse grass that clung to the sheer wall of dirt, sucking a precarious existence from the dry soil. The pathway dropped along the side of the cliff at breakneck speed, running higher and higher as they forced their way up to where the solid wall of pines marched grandly around the side of the mountains. From the look of it, there was no way of telling how recently this trail had been used. The solid rock would leave few hoofmarks for them to follow and they could only ride the trail to its end and then backtrack at first light if they had not come across anything definite which would give them a lead.

The steep slope soon began to tell on the horses and no amount of urging would make them increase their gait. There was water flowing at the bottom of the chasm which lay on their left and the cold dampness of it began to rise to them now that darkness had fallen. They had been on the ascent for more than two hours and Chris was beginning to feel the strain of it tell on him, and he thought that he heard other echoes of sound above the murmur of distant water and the muffled hoofbeats of their own mounts as they toiled slowly upward. Vague murmurs of sound that came up to them from the lower reaches of the trail, and others which seemed to sink from above them, from the broad, uprearing summits, still more than two thousand feet above their heads. He had the impression of the whole solid weight of the mountain crushing down on him from above. At a sharp bend in the trail, they stopped and sat loosely in the saddle, listening for the vague, indefinable sounds but unable to make anything of them. Chris still felt dissatisfied, then reached for his tobacco and rolled a smoke as he sat there, listening to the gale of his mount's breathing, loud in the stillness that clung about them. He held the match in his hand for a long moment, ready to light, then caught himself. The flare of a match could be seen for almost a mile, might bring a bullet. He put the match away again, nursed the dry smoke between his lips, getting no satisfaction from it, then moved ahead behind Denver.

The other seemed to know his way intimately, even in the pitch blackness that had descended on them. The night was bright with thousands of brilliant stars and there was the faint indication of moonlight far below them, but it did not shine on them, the vast bulk of the mountain shutting it off completely, hiding the moon from sight.

It was not until a couple of hours later that the moon finally drifted into sight directly ahead of them as they turned a wide bend in the trail, edging up to the timber belt. The black mass of the sky-rearing pines lay less than half a mile from them, dark and forbidding.

Denver pointed a finger upward. 'They must have taken the trail through the pines,' he said softly. 'It's the only way over this shoulder of the mountain and it would take the best part of a day to work around it. They wouldn't waste precious time like that, not with weary horses.'

'So we go ahead through the trees,' murmured Chris musingly. There was still the savage, bitter anger in him, coupled with a rising impatience. The long journey up into the mountain reaches had taken them the best part of six hours and all the time, there had been a memory in his mind which had haunted him every minute of the way. The memory of Diego's face when he had seen him in the sheriff's office, when the other had come to offer his help against Wilder. He had had the other at his mercy then, even though there were more than thirty of the Mexican's men drinking in the saloon. He ought to have put him into one of the cells along with Maxwell, or shot him down while he had had the chance. At that moment, he had been on equal terms with the other, which was more than could be said now.

The thought of Rosalie, riding with those two men threatened to swamp out everything else in his mind. They must have a tremendous lead on them by now, he thought grimly. Then he remembered that the others would have been forced to ride slowly up that treacherous and steep trail. He glanced sharply about him. This part of the trail was ideal for a bushwhacker.

'Good cover here for a dry-gulcher,' he said brusquely.

Denver snapped his head around. 'You figure they might lay for us along the trail?'

'Could be — one of them at least. If they reckon they're bein' followed, that's exactly what I'd expect Diego to do. He might decide to leave Maxwell behind to cover his trail while he rides on with the girl.'

Denver's gaze ran over the thick brush ahead of them. He pursed his lips and edged his mount forward a little, then paused and stared down at something in the rocks nearby. A moment later, he swung out of the saddle and went forward. Chris swung up to him, looked down with a feeling of excitement in him as the other bent and picked up something white, holding it up to him.

'Recognise this?' asked the rancher.

Chris took it, felt the smoothness of silk. Then he nodded quickly. 'It looks like one of Rosalie's handkerchiefs,' he said tensely. 'You figure she dropped it for us to see?'

'Sure looks that way to me,' murmured the other. He climbed back into the saddle. 'If she did, then it means we're on the right trail this time. Maybe we can make better time knowing that.' A quick glance at the trees and he went on quietly: 'There's goin' to be no dust yonder and the undergrowth will muffle the sound of the horses.' He seemed to have dismissed the idea of a bushwhacker lying in wait for them.

It was well into the early hours of the morning when they rode through into the heavy timber. Most of it was first-year pine, the trunks tall and straight for more than thirty feet before they spread out into a thick and impenetrable blanket over their heads, shutting out even the faint, shimmering starlight and the pale moonglow. The smell of moist earth was in their nostrils now and there was scarcely any sound all about them. Only the breathing of their horses disturbed the quiet stillness. Chris knew none of this land and yet he felt no inward concern. Denver obviously knew exactly where he was, had possibly ridden this particular trail on many occasions in the past.

They came out into the open a couple of miles further on; a wide break in the trees where the trail ran alongside a deep chasm, the ground falling away into pitch blackness on the very edge of the trail. As they came out into the open, Chris reined his mount. Far away, there was a single starved echo, fading swiftly. Denver turned in the saddle, looked across at him tightly.

'Sounded like a gunshot,' Chris said thinly. 'Far way.'

'Could be,' nodded the other.

'Trouble is that sounds are deceptive in the hills at night.'

Riding on, they listened for any repetition of the sound, but there was nothing more. The silence descended like a sable cloak all about them, the deep and utter silence of the mountains. The pines ran solemnly before them again, shutting out the rest of the world, rising in a flawless line towards the lower limits of the mountain crests. By degrees, the country became rougher. Huge boulders were scattered over the trail and they were forced to edge their way forward slowly and carefully, inching around the tall rocks, loose stones sliding under them and bouncing off down the slope. The trail seemed to hold to the crests of the ridges most of the way, then they were over its topmost point, dipping down again in a series of switchback courses to a levelling off place among the tall hills. Here the rocks were so numerous, dotting the slopes, the brush so thick among them, that Chris knew that if either of the two men had stayed behind to cover the trail, this was surely where it would be.

★   ★   ★

The going was tough now, really tough, and in some places, Maxwell and Diego had to dismount and lead their horses and the girl's through the sharp-edged boulders that studded the trail, where it twisted and wound in a series of almost terrifying curves towards the narrow, rocky valley that lay surrounded entirely by the tall mountains.

Rosalie was kept in the saddle all of the time, her body bruised and sore. They had ridden all night without a stop, Diego forcing them on with muttered curses whenever Maxwell suggested that they should halt, if only for a little while to give the horses a chance to blow and get their wind. He seemed to have now become obsessed by the idea of getting to their destination as quickly as possible, regardless of the discomforts they were forced to endure on the way.

Maxwell rode the short stretches of the trail in silence now, his flabby features twisted into a permanent scowl. Rosalie guessed that he was never a brave man even at the best of times — certainly he had shown nothing of courage during the time he had been sheriff — and he seemed to be on the very edge of panic now, his nerves stretched almost to breaking point. She caught him glancing back over his shoulder more often now, as if certain that someone was following close on their heels, ready to exact retribution for what they had done.

Forcing away the little tremor of fear in her own mind, she wondered whether she might not be able to turn the other's increasing nervousness to her own advantage.

'They're not far behind, Maxwell,' she said softly. She saw the other whirl in the saddle, glaring back at her. 'And when they do catch up with you, nothing is going to save you.'

'Shut up,' snarled the other. He made a swift, instinctive move towards his gun, his face twisted in sudden savage fury. For a moment, the thought of killing her lived in his mind. Then he dropped his hand away. 'Keep ridin',' he snapped, 'and keep your mouth shut.'

Rosalie knew that she was courting disaster, but she had to keep on, trying to play one man against the other. If she didn't succeed in that, there was just the chance that she might slow down their pace and allow anyone who might be following their trail a chance to catch up on them before they reached their destination.

'You know that Ranson is following you, don't you,' she went on remorselessly as the other reined his mount, moving up beside her, his face contorted with fury. 'And it's only a matter of time before he catches up with us. Then you're as good as dead and — '

'Damn you, I warned you to shut

up!' snarled Maxwell. His right hand clawed to draw the gun from its holster. It had half cleared the leather when the sound of a shot drove everything from the girl's mind. Maxwell reeled back in the saddle, clawing at his smashed wrist.

'I do not warn you again, *amigo*.' Diego thrust the smoking gun back into its holster. His face hard, he swung on Rosalie. 'As for you, *señorita*, I shall not hesitate to tie you to the horse and gag you if you try anything like that again.'

The girl recognised the menace in his tone, knew that he would do exactly as he said and fell silent, pressing her lips tightly together. But even as she rode forward again, aware of the murderous glance that Maxwell gave her, she felt an inward thrill of exultation. If Chris was following, if he was anywhere within ten miles at that moment, he would surely have heard the sound of that shot, echoing from the hills and mountains . . .

* * *

Dawn greyed the eastern heavens as they moved out of the pines and on to a stretch of rough trail. Here and there, it was possible to make out the marks of horses and men in the dust, recent marks, where the men had been forced to dismount and lead their horses.

'They can't be far ahead now,' murmured Denver. He lifted himself high in the saddle and glanced down into the narrow valley that opened out in front of them.

'You know this place at all?' Chris asked tautly.

'Heard about it,' corrected the other. 'Used to be some old mine workings in this part of the territory. Worked out long before the war. Nobody comes here now, except for men like Diego. Makes a good retreat for any *hombre* who's running from the law.'

'Sounds like just the sort of place Diego would head for,' agreed Chris. 'Like you said, a couple of men with

288

plenty of ammunition could hold off a whole army here. How do you figure on getting close enough to 'em for a killin' shot?'

'There are plenty of short trails in these parts. I doubt if Diego knows 'em all. But it'll be rough ridin' and in places we'll have to climb without the horses.'

'But you reckon we can come on 'em unawares?' Chris eyed the other closely.

Denver hesitated, then nodded slowly. 'I reckon so,' he agreed. 'Trouble is that they may be watchin' this part of the trail. If they are, they could spot us long before we get down into the valley.'

They made their way forward over some of the roughest footing that Chris had ever encountered. In several places, they were forced to dismount and lead their horses, breaking forward through tangled vine undergrowth, working their way around vast boulders and great masses of fallen rocks and earth. New slides of dirt were everywhere, blocking the trail in several places and it was here that they found the signs they were looking for; three horses had come this way very recently, certainly not more than a few hours before. Denver nodded in satisfaction.

'Like I figured,' he said softly, 'they're evidently headed for the old mine workings. Once they hole up in there, we'll have a job to smoke 'em out without runnin' the risk of shootin' the girl.'

'My guess is that Diego will leave Maxwell there to keep an eye on the girl and then head back to town.'

'Why do you reckon he'll do that?' asked the other. 'He'd be a hell of a sight safer here.'

'Sure he would. But somehow, he has to get back to make sure that I carry out my part of the bargain, even though it's certain that he won't keep his. Once I sign that place over to him, you can be sure that he'll kill the girl. His life won't be worth a plugged nickel from then on. He'll have to get rid of me if he's to take over the ranch and run it with his own men.'

Denver nodded his head bleakly. In the pale dawn light, his grey hair glistened under the wide-brimmed hat. 'I get your point, Chris,' he said tightly. 'So we have to take care of 'em both here?'

'That's right. We've got no other choice. If we can drop Diego when he rides out of the mine workings, it'll mean that we have only Maxwell to take care of and he'll be a scared man by now.'

'And if Diego sends Maxwell into town, refusing to risk his own skin, and stays with the girl himself?'

'Then we may have to alter our plans.' Chris clamped his teeth tightly together until the muscles of his jaw lumped under his flesh. 'Right now, our problem is to get sufficiently close to them without being spotted.'

★　★　★

A mile from the old workings, Diego reined his mount, grasped the saddle, and leaned back, staring along the way they had come. From where they were, it was possible to see for several miles along the winding, twisting trail that led back up the bleak side of the mountain. The pale light of the early dawn picked out the shapes and angles of the rocks, the rising spires of the mesas, silhouetted against the slowly, brightening heavens.

The feeling that maybe Maxwell was right and Ranson had decided to follow them after all, had been growing within him during the past three hours. As he sat there, he recalled the moment along the trail when he had been forced to shoot the gun from Maxwell's hand before he could shoot the girl. The sound of that single shot would have carried many miles back along the trail and he cursed himself soundly for not having realised that before. Narrowing his eyes, he peered back into the dim distance, trying to pick out anything that moved along the trail, any cloud of dust which would indicate that they were being pursued. He could see nothing, but his uneasiness did not fade. Instead, the tightness in his mind crystallised swiftly into a near certainty.

'Somethin' wrong?' muttered Maxwell sullenly.

'Just checkin',' murmured the other evenly. He glanced back in the direction of the small cluster of shacks which marked the position of the old mine workings. 'Could be that you were right when you figured Ranson might try to follow us. I think we should be careful and watch the trail, just in case.'

'You said yourself there wasn't anythin' to be afraid of, that Ranson would never dare to follow so long as we have the girl.'

Diego nodded. There was a bright, cold glitter in his eyes as he glanced at the other speculatively, let his gaze wander from the man's bloodied wrist, then back to his face again. 'I figure you could use a rifle, even with that wrist of yours,' he said softly, 'and I want to make sure this time. Better take cover along this stretch of the trail where you can spot 'em some ways off. If they do head this way, drop 'em all. You understand?' His lips drew back in a tight smile. He ignored the girl's sudden, sharp gasp.

Swiftly, she swung on him. 'You can't do that!' she said quickly, the words tumbling over each other as she forced them out. Her face seemed drained of all colour as the knowledge of what the other intended to do penetrated her mind. 'You promised that if he made over the Ranson place to you and rode out of the territory, you would let me go.'

'So I did,' murmured the other. His smile broadened, grew more menacing. 'But I did not say that he could follow me. A man has to protect himself when anyone pursues him. I am merely taking precautions. If he is not following our trail, then there is nothing to worry about, is there, *señorita*. On the other hand, if he has disobeyed my orders and is trying to trail us, then I fear that I must have him killed. That would be a pity. It would mean that I shall have to get my men and take over the Ranson place by force, because some of the men there will fight, even if this man himself is dead.'

'You want me to dry-gulch anybody who comes along this trail?' muttered Maxwell thinly. 'If there are too many for me what — '

'There won't be,' snapped the other, wheeling his mount away. 'They wouldn't risk coming up with too many men. That would be taking too big a risk as far as the girl is concerned. Nail them all and then make your way to the mine workings where we will be.'

Maxwell waited for a long moment, staring dumbly at the Mexican and then, when there were obviously no further instructions forthcoming, he gave a low grunt and moved off into the rocks that overlooked the trail at that point. As he rode off, he slid the rifle from its scabbard, held it balanced over the saddle horn.

No sooner was he out of sight, than Diego leaned over, grabbed the bridle of Rosalie's mount, held it tightly in one hand, as he led them forward, around the tortuous, twisting bends in the trail. All the time, they moved downgrade and in places, the descent was so steep that only their weight in the saddles, prevented their horses from sliding headlong down the slope.

An hour later, they reached the mine workings. There were several wooden huts all clustered together in front of the sheer, rising wall of the mountain where the deep shafts had been driven into the solid rock. The rusted rails had not seen any movement of the wagons which now stood in a long line, for more than a score of years, and the deep silence of an abandoned place lay over everything there, causing a slight chill to come into Rosalie's mind, as she looked about her, eyes wide. The sun had risen now, but this part of the mountain still lay in shadow and the coldness of the night was in the air. Not until midday would the sun have worked its way around the outjutting lip of rock, shining on to this bare stretch of rocky ground.

Diego motioned her to alight, sat holding her bridle as she did so. Pain jarred through her as cramp seized her legs and she almost fell headlong with the sudden stabbing pain. Biting back the cry that rose unbidden to her lips, she drew herself up to her full height and faced the other as he swung down, slapping the horses on the rumps, sending them cantering towards the edge of the rocky plateau.

'There'll be food inside one of these shacks,' he said quietly. 'I reckon you ought to be able to rustle up some breakfast.' He eyed her soberly as she made to move forward, caught at her arm, fingers biting in as he pulled her around so that she faced him. 'And one thing, *señorita*. Do you hope that your friends will ride in and rescue you? If they succeed in getting past Maxwell — and he will shoot straight from ambush because he knows what waits for him back in town if he's taken alive — you will die before they can rescue you. I promise you that.'

She pulled sharply away from him, her eyes snapping. 'I might have known that you would do that, you — killer,' she said through thinned lips.

Lifting his hand, the Mexican struck her across the face. The impact of the blow sent her reeling and she almost fell, knocked off her balance. Backing away, she put a hand up to her cheek. Diego raked a cold stare over her. 'Now get some food ready.'

Stumbling, she made her way over to the largest of the wooden shacks. There was the musty odour of decay in the air as she thrust open the door and stepped inside. It assailed her nostrils, making her cough and choke. Diego came in close on her heels, slammed the door behind him and took up his position by the window, where he could look back along the trail and see all that went on along the whole length of the plateau.

As she worked, Rosalie felt the sinking sensation of defeat in her mind. The other seemed to have thought everything out, even before they had reached this place and the knowledge strengthened the idea in her mind that Diego had been planning this kidnapping for a long time, possibly from the moment that Chris Ranson had showed up in town and intimated that he would take over his grandfather's ranch and fight to hold it. But Diego had not gone at this thing blindly, as Matthew Wilder had, relying on brute force to achieve his ends. He had waited for his chance, had played his hand cunningly, striking where Chris would be hurt most. Now, it seemed, he had succeeded . . .

★　★　★

As they headed down into the valley, following the winding trail, Chris was especially alert, his hands very close to his gun butts. The chance of spotting any dry-gulcher's rifle before it spat death towards them from the piled-up rocks was pretty remote. This was an ideal place for a man to hide, to watch the trail and shoot down a man from under cover. He drooped his shoulders forward, forced himself to concentrate on the ground ahead.

There were no words between the two men now as they rode. It was as if both recognised that they were nearing the end of the trail, that the showdown lay just around the corner and at any moment all hell could break loose around them.

Half a mile further on, Denver stopped abruptly and motioned to Chris to halt as he slipped from the saddle and bent to examine the patch of dry ground in front of him, hunking forward on his haunches. Then he looked up, pointed at the dry, powdery earth.

'They stopped here for a while,' he

said tightly. 'There are plenty of marks and then one of 'em rode off in that direction — ' He pointed off into the rocks to the right, ' — while the other two went straight on along the trail.'

Thoughtfully, Chris glanced up into the rocks. Here they lay in tumbled confusion, piled high where they overhung the trail. 'You reckon that one of 'em moved off to cover the trail around here?'

'I'm pretty darned sure of it,' murmured the rancher. He eased the Colt from its holster, checked it carefully. He did not put it back, but held it in his hand, ready for instant use. 'I figure we ought to split up, trail him over those rocks. He's sure to be up there somewhere and I'm bettin' that it's Maxwell. Diego won't want to let the girl out of his sight for a single moment. She represents a lot to him.'

Chris gave a brief jerk of his head in answer. What the other said had the ring of truth about it and he had no doubt that this was indeed the case.

Bending, he moved over to the high wall of rock at the edge of the trail, peered up to where the first rays of the morning sun were throwing the rocks into light and shadow. Maxwell was somewhere up there, he thought grimly, waiting among the rocks for the chance to draw a bead on them, shoot them down without a chance to defend themselves. He recalled what he had told Denver shortly before they had set out from town. Once they came upon these men who had taken the girl, they would shoot them down in any way they could, even if it meant shooting them in the back or in the head, just so long as they killed them without giving them a chance to harm the girl. He knew that if it came to the point, he would go through with that, no matter how it went against the grain to shoot a man in the back without warning, but these murdering polecats deserved nothing better. He sucked air down into his lungs, let it go in short pinches. Denver had already slipped away into

302

the boulders, moving swiftly and silently with a surprising agility for a man of his age, climbing the steep side of the trail, working his way up and behind any man who might be up there watching the trail.

With a careful slowness, he began moving along the floor of the trail until he reached a narrow passage that led up through the rocks. Cool wind sifted down the natural channel as he edged forward, eyes alert, starting at every sudden sound or movement. Halfway along the channel, he pondered the wisdom of this move. If Maxwell was there, then he would have to draw the other's fire so that Denver might move in on him from behind.

He began moving laterally along the face of the nearer slope, looking for a gentler pitch and in the end he found one and made better progress. Pausing often to keen the dark shadows thrown by the low sun, he climbed upward, moving like a cat, smoothly and silently, in spite of the stiffness in his limbs and the tiredness that pervaded his whole body. He came out of the rocks at a point higher than where he reckoned any man would hide and a moment later, peering down, he spotted Maxwell, some distance below him, his back to him. The other lay on a flat rock, a rifle thrust out in front of him. He had evidently chosen the spot for its excellent and commanding view over the trail and it came to him then, even before he noticed the other's obvious nervousness, that Maxwell must surely have spotted them long before they had reached the trail immediately below him. Several times, the other lifted his head, peering down at the winding scar of the trail below him, trying to make out where they were. He clearly knew that they had stopped for some reason down there and he was obviously puzzled. Chris grinned savagely to himself, feeling the hot sunlight touch his neck and shoulders as he crouched down behind the rocks. Maxwell had not wanted to take any chances. He had deliberately withheld his fire during their approach along the trail, meaning to shoot them in the back once they had ridden past him. What he had not allowed for, had been the sharp eyesight of the rancher, the fact that Denver could read trail as well as any Indian and had seen quite clearly, written there in the dust, the story that had told, as plainly as any words, that he had left the trail and ridden up into the rocks.

Now Maxwell kept twisting his head in every direction, even glancing behind and above him at times, eyes flicking from side to side, warily, probing every shadow for anything that moved. Worse still, he had discarded the rifle and held his sixer in his hand. The rifle would have proved to be a more cumbersome weapon to use in a confined space and Chris had hoped that the other would have retained it, thereby giving Denver and himself the edge on him. A sudden movement over to his left attracted his attention. Glancing round, he made out the tall figure of the rancher as the other pulled himself up over the smooth rock, lay for a moment clearly getting his breath back before continuing. Swiftly, Chris's glance flickered back to Maxwell. The other had also heard the faint sound as Denver had pulled himself up over the outcrop of rock. He had swung round, the Colt held tightly in his hand, his finger on the trigger, every limb poised as he peered into the shadows among the rocks, trying to discover the source of the sudden sound.

Denver moved again, dragging himself forward. He had evidently come out on to a difficult part of the climb and was forced to heave himself up hand over hand, with his guns still in their holsters. Chris emptied his lungs in a sudden exhalation. Maxwell pushed himself up to his full height, swung to face Denver and lowered the muzzle of the gun on him. With a sudden start, Chris realised that the rancher must now be in full view of the other. The shot whiplashed at the very instant that he brought his own weapon to bear on the man below him. Dimly, he heard the shriek as the bullet richocheted off a rock. Then the Colt bucked and hammered in his own fist, twice, three times it was triggered. He saw Maxwell rear up on his toes, try to turn to face him. Then the other was smashed back by the solid, jarring impact of lead. His gun exploded once as he pressed down on the trigger with the last ounce of strength in his body but he was already going backward when he fired and the slug soared high into the air over his head as his body crashed against the rocky ledge at his back. For a moment, he hung there, then he overbalanced, his body falling down the steep slope, bouncing from one rocky ledge to another until it crashed with a sickening, bone-shattering thud on the trail below.

Slowly, Chris made his way towards Denver, leaping from one rock to another until he was level with the other. The rancher was just getting to his feet, rubbing his temple where an ugly bruise was beginning to show.

'Did he hit you?' asked Chris quickly.

'Nope. Guess I must have fallen and hit my head on the rock. But he came damned close to gettin' me. I never figured he was that close.'

'He must've seen us a mile back along the trail. He was lyin' there waitin' for us to move on and then he'd have shot us both in the back.'

They made their way down to the trail. Maxwell lay face-downward under cover of the huge overhangs. Going forward, Chris turned him over with his toe, stared down into the man's fleshy face. The lips were drawn back in a snarl almost of defiance, even in death.

'I reckon he must've quarrelled with Diego somewhere along the trail,' said Denver, pointing to the other's smashed wrist. 'That would likely be the shot we heard durin' the night, back along the trail.'

Chris nodded. 'Trouble is that Diego will have heard the shots and he'll know that Maxwell wasn't shootin' at shadows. He'll be ready for us, just in case we did get past Maxwell.'

Denver laughed harshly. 'Then we'll just have to show that we're smarter than he is, Chris.' He moved towards the horses still standing in the shadow of the rocks. Swinging up into the saddle, he led the way forward. The trail wound and dipped in front of them for another quarter of a mile and at the end of that time, they were able to sight the cluster of long wooden shacks that stood in front of a tall wall of solid rock, the ground there still in shadow.

'There are the shacks,' said Denver, nodding towards the mine workings. 'If I've guessed right then he'll be holed up in one of them. The only other thing he could do would be to move down the shaft into the rock.'

'You reckon it's likely he'll do that?' asked Chris.

'Nope, I don't reckon so. If he did that, there would be too many ways we could reach him without him being able to see us. Those workings go clear back into the rock for nearly a mile. But there's nothing at the end of 'em and if he went there we could sit tight and starve him out, and he ain't such a fool that he don't know that. In the shacks, he could pick us off quite easily if we tried to pet him.'

'So he's holed up in one of those shacks,' repeated Chris tautly. 'But that ain't goin' to help us none. There are probably half a dozen shacks there and he could be in any one of 'em. Not only that, but they seem to be built on some kind of plateau. It won't be a simple matter getting close enough to him, even if we do find out where he is. He could cover the whole stretch of ground from any one of those huts.'

'You're right. We have to circle around and come up against the rock face.'

'Can we do that?' Chris looked at the other in surprise. 'I thought you didn't know these parts.'

'Ain't been here myself, but I did

know an old miner once who worked these diggings. Told me quite a heap of things about this place. If what he said was true, there should be a hidden trail leading up to the rock wall at the back of those shacks.'

'And you reckon you can find it?' Chris felt a new hope beginning to stir in him at the other's words. If there was such a trail and they succeeded in getting behind Diego without the other being aware of it, then there was a good chance of taking the other by surprise before he had a chance to harm the girl. As it was, this was the only chance they had and he had to follow the other from there on.

They rode for another half mile before Denver reined his mount to a sudden halt. Chris glanced about him, but saw nothing out of the ordinary. Then the rancher pointed to their left. There was a narrow gap in the rocks on that side of the trail. To the casual eye, it would have passed unnoticed. But now that he came to look at it more closely, he saw that whereas it was little more than a two-foot wide gap in the rocks there, where it fronted the trail, it widened out appreciably only a few yards at the back of the rocks, formed a kind of natural wrinkle in the ground, a long chute of rock.

'We'll leave the horses here,' said Denver quietly. He slid from the saddle and waited for Chris to do likewise.

Rock caught at Chris's arms and shoulders as he squeezed through the gap in the rock. Passing around tall chunks of weather-carved stone, he discovered the trail that wound between the worn walls of sandstone and eventually, they came out on to an area of bald, open rock. Here, they made better time and the sun had scarcely climbed to the zenith when they came upon the sudden sharp turn and found themselves ascending once again. Directly ahead of them, clearly seen now, was the great rearing face of rock that stood at the back of the shacks they had noticed earlier from the main trail.

Chris brought his mind back to Diego as he followed Denver through the tumbled, massive boulders that thrust themselves up in front of them at every turn. He tried to put himself in the place of the other, tried to think out what Diego might do once he heard those shots from back along the trail, once he knew for sure that he had been trailed this far, even though he would not be certain whether Maxwell had stopped them or not. By now, he might be waiting for Maxwell to show up with news of what had happened. When he didn't show, he would know that Maxwell had been killed and that this part of his plan had somehow come unstuck. Would he decide that the girl was too great a liability to have around? Would he try to make a run for it, heading out for New Mexico, as far as possible from this place, hoping to keep one jump ahead of him, knowing what would happen if Chris managed to meet up with him?

Ten minutes later, they found themselves facing a sheer wall of rock that rose for the best part of a hundred feet in front of them, with not even a solitary handhold in sight.

'How do you expect us to climb that?' muttered Chris, staring up at the rock face that towered over them. 'There's no way up there.'

'But there has to be a way. That old miner was so sure that — '

'You think maybe that he was wanderin' a little when he spun you this yarn?' grunted Chris. 'Don't look to me like there's any way up.'

Denver walked along the base of the rock face, peering up, squinting against the glaring sunlight that was reflected from the smooth rock. He moved slowly to the far end, then turned and shook his head in puzzlement, began to move back. Halfway back, he paused, darted forward. Chris moved up to him, saw the opening in the rock, a sort of natural tunnel. Once, in some long past age, there had been a subterranean river here, flowing out of the solid rock and down into the valley which lay some hundreds of feet below them, a natural waterfall, washing its way down the rock. Now the river was gone, dried up these countless thousands of years, but the water course that it had laid was still there, set in the rock. The gap was wide enough and high enough for a man to stand with his head just touching the rocky roof of the tunnel.

Quietly, Denver said: 'This must be it. A natural tunnel that leads into one of the shafts. That's what he must have been talkin' about.'

Before Chris could stop him, he had plunged into the darkness of the tunnel, his head lowered. For a second, Chris stood there irresolute, then ducked his head and followed the other. The metallic sound of their boots on the hard rock struck vibrating echoes ahead of them. How long they moved forward, it was impossible to tell. The darkness here was absolute and they were forced to move on by sense of touch only. Rough outcrops of rock tore at their feet and hands until they were cut and bruised.

Denver stopped suddenly a while later, stopped so quickly that Chris bumped into him from behind.

'What is it?' he asked tightly, his voice carrying and echoing from the rocks.

'There's fresh air coming in from straight ahead,' murmured the other, his voice reaching back to Chris. 'That must mean that one of the main tunnels is only a little way ahead.' He began to move forward again and less than five minutes later, they were standing in one of the large mine shafts, the metal rails gleaming faintly in the pale glimmer of light that filtered into the workings from the opening less than fifty yards away.

Chris felt winded, his fingers bleeding from that long climb through the narrow tunnel. As they came out into the open, he felt the cold anger in his mind rise up until it threatened to choke him. The shacks were silent less than twenty yards away and from where they stood it was impossible to tell in which one Diego was hidden with the girl. Then there was a sudden movement close to the largest of the shacks. Slitting his eyes against the glare of the sky, he saw the Mexican move out, dragging the girl with him. The other was moving slowly in the direction of the trail, evidently wondering where they were, worried, but clearly confident that there was no one at his back. Crawling swiftly forward, Chris angled over the open ground towards the nearest hut, threw himself against it, the breath rasping harshly in his throat. He was not worrying about Denver now. Diego was to be his, although he knew the rancher was ready to back up any move he made.

His gun in his hand, he moved around to the edge of the shack, feeling the anger in him as he saw the other dragging the girl forward, then thrust her down behind one of the rocks which overlooked the end of the trail.

His teeth clenched and his eyes slitted against the glare, Chris moved out from behind the shack, the gun in his hand pointed at Diego's back as the other moved across towards one of the small gullies.

'Hold it there, Diego,' he called sharply. He saw both the girl and the Mexican whirl at the sudden sound of his voice. For a moment, there was a look of stunned, incredulous surprise written all over the Mexican's swarthy features. Then he dived for the rocks, gripping his gun and bringing it up to cover, not Chris, but the girl. Triggering the Colt, Chris saw Diego stagger and jerk as the slug took him in the shoulder, knocking him to one side. The girl had thrown herself down, aware of her danger, and the slug which had been intended for her, whined harmlessly off the rock close to her head, showering her with chips of stone.

Even though he had been hit, Diego was far from finished. Rolling over on his side, he brought up his weapon again, loosed off a couple of shots at Chris. Something scorched along Chris's upper arm and he gritted his teeth as the burst of agony ran up into his shoulder. Somehow, he managed to steady himself, levelling the gun on the prone body of the Mexican. The hammer fell only once but it was enough, Diego tried to get to his feet, tried to hold life in his eyes and hand long enough to get off another shot, but the gun slipped from his nerveless hand and clattered on to the hard rocks in front of him a split second before he toppled forward on to his face and lay still, a motionless figure in the hot sunlight that was just beginning to show around the tall edge of the mountain.

The gun smoke cleared slowly as Chris went forward to where the girl lay against the rock. Denver came over from the mouth of the mine workings and stood looking down at Diego's body for a long moment. Then he shook his head slowly and moved over to them, his face grim.

'I reckon it's all finished.' said the rancher slowly. 'Without Diego, his men will ride on over the hill and never come back. He was all there was to hold them together. Wilder's finished too. He'll hang for sure.'

Chris nodded, placed his arm around the girl, felt the warmth of her against him. There was a feeling in his mind that he had just woken from some terrible nightmare to find that it had all been nothing more than a dream and that life was good and fresh and clean again. Together, the three of them made their way down the winding trail to where the horses were waiting less than a quarter of a mile away..